# UNDER THE PINES

## A NOVEL

Jennifer Bisbing

ISBN-10: 0692634444
ISBN-13: 978-0692634448

Cover and book design by Registered Creative

Author photo by Emma Bilyk

Manufactured in the United States

First Edition

*This book is dedicated to the trees on my Sunday hikes, the exposed pines of my lofted 100-year-old coach house, the carved oaks in my inherited antique desk, the sturdy cypress out my retreat window, and the trees in the paper that hold these words.*

# 1

## Rust Murders

Fish jumped in the distance. Their splashes carried across the emptiness of the large field. The river wasn't in sight, but from the faint hiss of rushing water, she knew it was close. She saw herself surrounded by tall, dry rustling grass, soon to become tumbleweed. As morning broke, sunshine hit the grass, its dead stalks translucent as amber, rendering the field fiery gold. Squinting into the sun, she noticed several men gathered in the distance, standing across from looming leafless oaks filled with large birds.

She started running towards the group of people, but the sharp grass scraped at her clothing, slowing her down. The ground had begun to freeze and harden in uneven ways making it nearly impossible for her to keep her footing. Every few steps she stumbled over woodchuck mounds. Then she tumbled over something larger than a mound of dirt, landing facedown on the cold, hard earth. With her face squished into the ground, she smelled rotting leaves and dead grass intermingled with stale cigarette. She lifted her head and saw deer casually meandering past, unfazed by her noisy fall.

When she returned to her feet, a breeze, with a chill of winter, picked up speed across the open field. She wanted to get closer to the people, to the commotion. Then a lop-eared mangled rabbit darting past abruptly stopped her. When she turned to follow it, she was blindsided by the wind, which carried an overwhelming scent of death.

Josie woke up, gasping for air and sat up in bed. Immediately after she opened her eyes, the phone rang downstairs, though it was the middle of the night. "Who's dead?" she yelled out her bedroom door.

The orange tabby cat, named Tabby, jumped off the bed with a loud thump and scampered down the stairs. Josie often wondered if she should have given Tabby a more creative name. She was a faithful, clever friend and deserved better. But there was no time to think about that now.

Josie followed Tabby downstairs. Her mother and father were up and headed towards the phone, question marks on their sleep-scrunched faces. Her grandmother had advanced cancer, and they all feared this might be bad news from the hospital.

They only had one phone — it was dingy yellow and hung on the olive-colored kitchen wall, high above Josie's reach. When all of them reached the kitchen they found the cat circling beneath the phone, rubbing her whiskered cheeks against the long cord. Josie and her mother sleepily hovered nearby while her father picked up the receiver.

"Hello?"

"Herman, this is Patrick Dusek from Operations. We have a request for your team at a 901 crime scene near Rust."

Josie's father fanned his hand, shooing them away when he heard the dispatcher on the line. A sense of relief filled the room. Someone was dead, but it wasn't her grandmother. Lethargically Josie's mother gently guided her back upstairs to her bedroom, with the cat at their heels. "Try to get some sleep, honey. You have school again on Monday and you won't be able to sleep in." Her mother tucked in the bright purple covers up to Josie's chin.

Josie tossed and turned, wiggling out of the tucked-in blankets, as she listened to her father's heavy footsteps downstairs as he prepared to head out to the crime scene. Her dad a tall, broad-shouldered man with a thick mumble, worked for the Michigan State Police at the Bridgeport Regional Laboratory. His somber manner was the only clue that he had seen things in his line of work that most people only see fictionalized on TV or film. He had walked and talked with the dead, trying to decipher whose shoes had stepped where, when no one was watching. He had found clues in the cracks where murderers neglected to clean. He had located palm prints and fingerprints on walls thieves didn't remember touching. He had seen what someone can do with a knife on human flesh and knew how to prove which knife had done the cutting.

The phone rang often in the middle of the night, and the startling ring usually served as a trigger for Josie to have a series of wild dreams and nightmares. Her father could be gone for days working on cases, which exacerbated Josie's vivid dreams, frequently causing night terrors when she was younger. Lately, he had tried not to stray too far out of range from the Flint hospital where his mother was in intensive care, but Josie overheard him tell her mother that this murder was all the way in Rust.

Josie had never heard of Rust. It didn't even sound like the name of a town. She couldn't recall driving through or knowing any family from there. Needing to know where Rust was she flicked on the light and rustled through some papers under her bed, pulling out a Michigan road map. When she found Rust on the map, she muttered, "Way up there above the National Forest. Dad will never take me to see that crime scene." Josie picked up her markers and began marking the map. With several bright colors she labeled the places she had been according to vacation, family, crime scene, pit stop on a road trip, or hope to see. She had an elaborate diagram distinguishing what the different colored markers stood for. Most of the crime scenes she had seen were old ones that her father had worked on while still at the Lansing Police Post. On vacations they would often visit them. Usually it was just a house or a field that didn't look much different from any other place. But the graphic details her father recounted from each crime fascinated Josie. She drew a big red circle around Rust.

⌐

Josie finally fell asleep as, miles away, her father, Herman and two other criminologists, Sergeant Greg Adams, a latent print specialist, and Dean Madison, a serologist, headed north along Highway 33. The fall morning brought a light smattering of yellow honey locust leaves on their windshield. Herman was tempted to turn on the windshield wipers to disperse them, but the blades squeaked, and he thought it would only add to the tension inside the car.

He clutched the wheel with both hands, as this stretch of 33 grew narrower and turned to gravel. Dawn's empty, wide-open, crimson sky — plus the silence in the car, which was only interrupted sporadically by nervous small talk between his new co-workers — filled the station wagon with a strange anxiety. There was always some uneasiness prior to arrival at a scene. First it was the uncertainty of finding the scene and what they would encounter. Further there was the niggling worry that if the local cops had not preserved everything properly, then their carefully collected evidence risked being thrown out of court. This case involved the added stress that the crime scene was on an unmarked dirt road with only power lines guiding them to the location. And it didn't help that they had all consumed too much coffee from Dean's thermos.

## Rust Crime Scene

It was a typical dump spot, a dark, cold, lonely place, with a couple of troopers guarding the scene, shivering in their patrol car. As the Bridgeport crew got out of their station wagon, one of the local police officers walked up quickly.

"Good to see you guys, finally," he said. "Follow me. The body is over here."

The local police and Lab crew approached the body and then moved upwind from the stench. Young victims and cold mornings heighten the senses, Herman thought. He had no sense of smell. I hope none of them vomit before I can get these footprints cast, Herman worried as they all took a close look at her bruises. Herman's pulse was a bit faster than normal, and he had a slight case of the shakes. He remembered his doctor saying he should cut down on the coffee. Too late this morning for that, Dean must have put rocket fuel in his coffee, and really what do doctors know, he thought. After that visit, Herman promised himself he would avoid doctors the rest of his life.

Herman and the other examiners were dressed in suits and thick overcoats, normal attire for all government jobs at that time even if you were digging around in the dirt. Greg and Dean took deep breaths as they turned away from the body and headed back to the station wagon to grab the gear. There was a bit of grumbling about the cold, something Midwesterners did every autumn even though this was only a minor dip in the thermometer, and it was the same temperature that would bring them out in shorts in April.

When they approached the local police again, Herman overheard them discussing a pet rabbit that was hiding next to the body when she was found, seemingly ignoring the fact that they were standing next to a strangled girl. Herman couldn't care less about the rabbit and focused on the space surrounding the dead teenager. He instructed them all to step back. As they complied, the dry grass beneath their feet filled the quiet with a boisterous crunch.

He first cast the footprints that didn't appear to be the standard Michigan State Police-issued boot. There was a tennis shoe-looking print that had an unusual cutting pattern. As the casts dried he studied the body noticing that her long hair was frozen stiff into the grass and her body was twisted in an unnatural position. She must have been strangled while standing up, Herman thought, and then fallen to the ground when he finally let go of his hold on her neck.

He found a faint footprint on the victim's white nylon jacket. The print was small, but left a distinct imprint of dirt on the jacket fibers. Being new to this Lab, Herman was teased by Greg and Dean that he would never get a match from that speck of dirt. Disregarding their skepticism, Herman photographed the markings and then put clear plastic tape over the tiny print to preserve it. He told Greg and Dean they would have to wait and see, but they still persisted. "Herman, I think you are being overzealous," Dean said. Herman had to entertain the critical thoughts of the other scientists at his new Lab. But he wasn't sure that they were the type of people that could uphold the high level of integrity or follow strict ethical guidelines, which were required of forensics scientists. Herman was always trying to advance forensic science; never quite feeling satisfied with the current Department standards. He could see that this print was a unique piece of evidence, since no one else would step on the victim's jacket but the killer. Even cops hate getting that close to dead bodies.

⟵

At home on Sparrow Street, Josie was propped up with several pillows in a living room chair, reading her new Nancy Drew book, as her mother got ready to leave for work. After draining the last of her overly sweetened coffee, her mother hurried out the front door saying, "Be good, Josephine. Now don't forget to go next door for dinner. Aunt Caroline is fixing your favorite." Josie crinkled up her nose as if she'd smelled something bad.

The phone rang right after Josie's mother pulled out of the driveway and the cat ran into the kitchen in a hurry. Her mother had told her never to answer unless it rang only twice, two times in a row. This time it rang three times, twice in a row. Josie wondered if her mom had said two or three times. She wasn't sure what to do. So the third time it started ringing, she scooted a chair underneath the phone and hopped up to reach the receiver. There was a strange woman's voice asking if her father or mother were home. Josie had been instructed to lie when someone asked that exact question. "They're home, but not available," Josie replied in a polite but firm voice. The woman on the phone insisted that she speak with them because it was an emergency. To Josie, emergencies always meant someone was dead.

"Is someone dead?" Josie asked matter-of-factly. The woman nervously said she would try Josie's father's work number. "But..." Josie tried to tell the woman that he was at a crime scene, but the caller had hung up.

⸺

Back in Rust, the police radio started crackling and Herman heard his name. The Bridgeport Regional Laboratory Lab Director was calling to tell him his mother wasn't doing well, and he should hurry to Flint. He leapt into the state's station wagon and started it up with the back gate open. Then he hopped out flustered realizing that they only had one Lab vehicle for the whole team, and the examiners needed the supplies in the back. He shouted, "I need a ride." A trooper yelled back, "No problem," and motioned for Herman to follow him to his car across the field.

By radio, the troopers formulated an elaborate plan of relaying Herman back to Bridgeport in a series of state patrol cars. Channel two of the radio grumbled on as troopers tried to figure out the best drop off and pick up locations. Herman complained about how he would miss the autopsy, and he wasn't sure the other guys would handle the victim's jacket okay. The trooper repeatedly told him not to worry — his mother was more important. This annoyed

Herman since he needed to think about anything other than his mother.

With flashing lights and at top speeds, the troopers took Herman to one Regional State Post after another, switching cars and drivers, until he reached Bridgeport Regional Laboratory, where he picked up his own state car. He circled back to Saginaw to pick up Josie. His wife was already at the hospital sitting frozen and clutching Herman's mother's pale hand. She had gone early that morning before heading to work, not even knowing about the call.

Josie was startled to see her father walk through the front door, and was thankful she didn't have out all of her secretly gathered forensic supplies. She was still in her polka dot pajamas, but without even looking at her, Josie's father instructed her to hop in the car.

"Hurry up!" he demanded while holding the doorknob. "We need to get to the hospital." Josie grabbed her boots and hat, but didn't have time to put them on as her father pushed her along. As they went out the front door the cat tried to sneak out and Herman gave her a firm shoo, then Tabby ran to hide. Josie hated the way he treated her cat, but in this instance, she thought her dad's anger was probably because Tabby sensed Herman's mother was dying. Tabby loved his mother, never leaving her lap when she visited. Plus Herman seemed jealous of the attention his mother gave the cat. In his eyes, cats were just animals and didn't deserve such coddling.

Josie sat in the back seat of the state car, which was utilitarian and definitely smelled different compared to the new Monte Carlo her mother was driving. In the Monte Carlo, Josie had stashed maps and drawings, and there was a flashlight that her mother left in the car for emergencies. She frequently told Josie not to waste the batteries reading in the dark.

In the state car, reeking like bleach, Josie began to look under the floor mats and in the cracks of the seats for any trace evidence from murder scenes. "Stop fussing around back there," Herman demanded. "This isn't our property."

The car was parked every night in their driveway, and Josie wondered how it could be someone else's property. The old patrol car had been repainted, but the huge State Police logo on the side door was still visible through the cheap paint job and something every visitor noticed. Josie didn't talk about her father being a science-cop much. Although she would have loved to tell everyone that her father solved crimes, her mother told her it made some people nervous. Josie thought only the guilty ones.

Herman was on channel two, the closed-circuit police radio, talking about the case with the examiners, who were on the road and headed towards the morgue for the autopsy. He asked what other evidence had been found, holding down the CB knob, then releasing it and waiting for an answer. "Not much else, Herman. The locals found the rabbit, slightly beaten up like the person who killed the girl tried to extinguish the only witness. We searched for evidence all the way to the river and back. Combed through the surrounding tall grass about a half-mile in both directions. One direction seemed to have mashed grass as if someone fell while running. It didn't lead anywhere though. Just a cigarette butt that seemed too old for this fresh body." Flustered Herman slammed the receiver back into the clip.

Josie thought it was odd that her dream had included all of those things. I remember that cigarette smell now, she thought. She had to tell her dad about it. "Dad! My dream…" "Dad, I want to tell you about my dream… Dad? Dad." There were long pauses in between Josie's calls to her father from the backseat. He seemed lost in his thoughts. Josie gave up and sat back and reminisced, I wanted to help that bunny. I want a bunny.

"Yes, Josie," her father finally said as he picked up the Motorola receiver, "Thanks guys for the update. Good luck with the autopsy."

Josie decided to drop the dream since he seemed mad. "Dad, can't we turn on the police light and speed there?" she said with excitement.

"This isn't official state business, Jo."

"Sure it is, you're an official state science-cop with a badge, and we have business to attend to." Josie said while nervously bobbing up and down on the spongy seat.

"Okay, Josie. We'll use your logic if I get written up. And don't tell your mother we did this."

"I won't." Josie smiled. Her father switched on the flashing light and Josie burst into laughter and excitement. "Let's go, Dad!"

Herman sped up and swiftly began passing cars. When he realized how fast he was going he pulled over and asked Josie to sit in the front and put on the lap belt. There were no seatbelts in the backseat. The front ones were flimsy, but better than nothing, Herman thought. Josie always felt older while sitting up front with her father — almost part of the police force, though she could barely see over the enormous dashboard. Lost in the rush and excitement of the high speed, she forgot they were headed to see her sick grand-mother. She leapt up to her knees, wiggling out of the lap belt when she saw her favorite roadside farm stand. When she saw all the pumpkins and shouted, "Can we stop for hot cider?" But her father's expression suggested he had not forgotten where they were going.

When they arrived at Hurley Hospital, her father marched along a few feet in front of Josie. His legs were so long that he had a habit of walking a few paces in front of everyone in the family. Josie's mother constantly complained she couldn't keep up and that he was always "leaving them behind." Unfazed by being left behind, Josie trotted to meet her dad at the information desk, while looking wildly around the emergency room to see what sorts of accidents had brought other people there.

The last time they all visited the hospital, there was a man sitting in the waiting room with a huge gash on his forehead. Josie's mother had tried to shield her from it, but Josie had a bunch of questions and actually ended up wandering over to the man when her parents weren't looking. She received a firm scolding for talking to strangers — a habit her mother was trying to break her of. Her father's constant lecturing that someone might kidnap her if she didn't stop it only intrigued Josie more.

She often wondered what it would be like to be kidnapped. Which one of the strangers would be a potential kidnapper? She wanted to learn how to distinguish the bad guys from the good guys. Currently she had a tendency to like everyone. She also wondered if her father would find her, and would the whole police force come out looking for her, even the dogs? Like her father, Josie was fascinated with people's tragedies. She wanted to solve crimes. How did they catch them? She thought if I was kidnapped, what better way to help solve the case? I'd have all the facts. Plus the police would know my dad already had my fingerprints and hair samples to be used for comparison with traces found in places where I was held hostage.

Josie was lost in thought, scanning the waiting room when her father tugged on her arm and held it, so that she would keep up as they went down the hall. They entered her grandmother's room, and her mother jumped out of the chair tucked next to the bed.

"She doesn't have her wig on! Josie has never seen her without hair."

Josie peeked around her father's wide leg and saw a bald version of her grandmother. "Can I touch her head?" Josie said. Her mother sighed and glared at her father.

"Come here, Josie. You can help me put on her wig. She wouldn't want to wake up and have you see her like this."

"The doctor said she isn't going to wake up this time. Can't we stop with the charades?" Herman said in a firm voice. "Let's just be with her."

Josie's mother came around the bed to comfort Herman. Josie sneaked a touch of her grandmother's bare head as her mother buried her face into her father's chest, taking big sips of air in between tiny sobs. Her grandmother's head was smooth and chilly. Josie took off her winter hat and put it on her grandmother and crawled into bed with her. Her grandmother stirred and opened her soft hazel eyes. "Sweet Josie," she said in a soft, shaky voice. "Mind your dreams." Her grandmother closed her eyes again as Josie's father and mother hovered and asked if she needed anything.

"What did she say?" Her father asked.

Josie shrugged and looked scared. "I think she said, 'Mind your dreams.' I don't know what that means."

Her mother reached for Josie and said, "That's okay. We don't need to know what it means."

The heart-monitoring machine starting making beeping noises and Josie yelled out, "What does that mean?" Nurses and doctors immediately rushed in, fussing and listening to her grandmother's heart and asking her if she could hear them while Josie was still on the bed clutching her grandmother's arm. Josie's mother stood frozen and helpless even though she had resuscitated several patients while working at another hospital. Within what seemed like only seconds after the beeping began, one doctor turned to Herman and said, "She is gone. I'm so sorry."

Herman stood still like a tree trunk as his wife Martha tried to hug him. One of the doctors gently started guiding Josie off of the bed. "But I want to be with her," Josie protested as the doctor tried to help her down. Martha began to sob, and Herman grabbed Josie, picked her up, and marched out of the room. Martha was left alone with Herman's mother and had to run to catch up.

"I want her back." Josie cried out.

"She's not gone." Herman said with a shaky voice. He cleared his throat and continued, "She *is* alive in you. My mother's cells are living in you," he said in a firm professional tone.

Tears flowed down Josie's cheeks. "I don't understand."

"Herman, give her to me." Martha demanded. "You're scaring her even more. You don't always have to be a scientist. She needs a father."

Herman huffed as Josie wiggled down out of his arms. "My mother just died and you're bitching at me," he shot back, turning towards the door. Josie could only watch as his strides got longer and his blurry frame disappeared through the exit.

# 2

"Stop biting your nails. You don't want to leave your finger-nails everywhere." Josie stopped biting immediately and looked up at her dad. "You never know what will end up being a crime scene," Herman said to Josie as they pulled into the Walter J. McHenderson funeral home parking lot.

These people here are already dead and no one is going to kill someone while they're visiting a dead person. That would be just too much, Josie thought, but kept it to herself.

"Now stay close. We just need to pick out a casket and sign some papers. I don't want you wandering off." Herman said as they got out of the car. Josie nodded and took big steps to keep up. With light leaps she joyfully counted the blocks of sidewalk, "One, two, three, four, five."

"What are you counting Josie?" Herman asked sounding annoyed. He was trying to remember if it had been two or three days since his mother's death. He scolded himself that he should have taken care of all these funeral details before. Now everything was going to be rushed. Herman didn't wait for Josie's answer. He shooed her inside the ornate double doors of the funeral home.

Josie's eyes widen when she entered. "This looks like a castle," she said softly.

With amazement Josie gazed around the old stone building, which had once been a mansion, and imagined fancy people living in the extravagant rooms. She wondered if the McHenderson's lived here at some time and that's how it got its name or if the guy her father was shaking hands with was Walter. Although she had told her dad she would stay close, Josie was determined to find out where they were hiding her grandmother. She had a few questions to ask her about the vivid dreams she had been having. Josie thought she looked dead when she spoke last time, and she just might do it again.

While viewing the caskets, Josie had the urge to climb into them to see how each one felt. To her the half-opened boxes looked like bobsleds with fluffy sleeping bags tucked inside. But she thought that they looked too small for her grandmother, who was a tall woman compared to the other old ladies Josie knew. She wanted to make sure there was plenty of room for her grandmother's big feet, but she figured trying to climb in and out without being seen would be too risky. So she kept quiet and slowly let her father get farther ahead of her in the showcase rows.

Without drawing attention to herself Josie peered around corners looking for a door resembling a private entrance to wherever they were keeping her grandmother. She knew she had to be quick. Once the funeral director mentioned money, since her father always got agitated when money was discussed, it would be a perfect time to bolt. But she also knew she had to be patient because there was sure to be a long story before the money talk — Herman never could resist talking about his mother.

What Herman frequently told others about his mother was surprising, because most other people spoke of her psychic abilities. There was a loving tone and pride in Herman's voice as he told the director, "My mother is — well, *was* — a classic 1950s housewife and the solid foundation in our family. She did all of the laundry nearly daily with my brother and I playing so many sports."

"Will your brother be here this evening as well?"

"No. My mother also ironed anything that could wrinkle — even my father's handkerchiefs. She did all of the cleaning including compulsively vacuuming, once my father had splurged on a nice Hoover. She regularly polished all the wood floors to the point where they were almost too slick to walk across." There was a nearly inaudible, "I see" from the funeral director, who did not look like a Walter to Josie but maybe his son.

"She did all of the cooking and hosting for the holidays. She hosted tea parties, and planned and prepared all of our frequent family picnics. She hosted dinner parties for friends and members of our church, too. She was a social butterfly and everyone loved her. She cooked classic German food. She cooked what her mother taught her to cook, though it could've used a few more spices. The only chore I don't remember her doing alone was shopping. She never drove or had a checking account, so my father went everywhere with her. My mother dedicated her life to being a mom. She mothered everyone she met. There isn't a person I know who has anything bad to say about my mother. Not even the other women that she repeatedly beat playing a game of Bridge."

"She sounds like she was a lovely woman. I'm so sorry for your loss," the director said while steering Herman around the caskets.

"Now if you want to hear about my father, that's a whole other story. He was strict. He lived by a set of rules, ones he learned from his father, which he enforced on my brother and me. I'm not sure if his set of rules were any harsher than other children's experiences in the 1950s, but in our house, there was little tolerance for errors. He had a heart attack the first time my mother was diagnosed with cancer. I think it didn't fit into his life plan."

They had just finished the second lap around all the caskets and before Herman went on to say more about his dad, the funeral director tactfully interrupted and said, "Well, this one will run you…" Josie turned around and headed towards a narrow hallway that looked uninviting, unlike the other colorfully decorated rooms with flowers and soft lighting. She slowly opened the door at the end of the hall and looked down a steep set of stairs. She wasn't sure how they could get the bodies down there or back up, but she headed down anyway.

Basements meant spiders. She looked closely before placing her hand on the railing. The last time she was in her own basement she put her hand right on a spider crawling up the railing and ended up falling down the stairs after having jumped with fright. She couldn't make that mistake again and still sneak down to find her grandmother.

It was quiet and chilly in the basement, which prompted Josie to note how cold it had been upstairs too. "To avoid rotting," she whispered. At the bottom of the stairs, she peered around a corner and saw a row of bodies, neatly lined up and in different stages of dress. Most of them had on pants or underwear. Josie giggled and wondered why they needed underpants?

Mom always said you need to wear clean underpants in case you have to go to the hospital and a see doctor, Josie recalled. No one was going to see these people, and they wouldn't be going to the bathroom either. They were going to be sealed in a coffin and put in the dirt. Clean underwear didn't matter underground.

She saw her grandmother — shirtless with her chest covered by a utility-looking towel. Her surgically removed breasts must have made the embalmer uncomfortable. It was a topic no one talked about, but Josie had always felt their absence whenever she curled up in her grandmother's arms.

She stepped closer past several embalmed bodies that looked like they were sleeping, very still, with lots of makeup on their faces. Josie kept repeating the phrase; "I am safe and free," which her grandmother had told her to say v she was scared. As she approached her grandmother, a man shouted, "Hey! What are you doing down here?"

Josie didn't flinch or look in his direction. She was still focused on walking towards her grandmother. "I need to ask my grandmother something."

"Well, she won't respond. And you can't be down here."

"I'll be quick. She's right here." Josie briefly stared at her grandmother's unusually puffy face and then whispered in her ear, "Please come visit me in my dreams and tell me what they mean." Suddenly the room got even colder.

"You're upsetting them by talking to them like that — they need to be accepted as dead," the man said "Go! Now!" Josie ran towards the stairs. She could feel something strange was happening.

Josie flew up the stairs, rounded the corner from the hall into the showcase room and ran right into the funeral director's large legs. She stood frozen as he stared down at her. Then she heard her father's voice, business-like still asking questions, he wasn't mad. Josie let out a boisterous exhale. He must not have known she was gone, but the director did. And he wasn't going to take his eyes off her now, which wasn't to his advantage since Herman didn't like men looking at his daughter. He had worked on enough child murder and molestation cases not to trust any man around his own daughter.

Herman hurried the director along, interrupting with an insistent "no" each time he tried to add a new expense onto the arrangements. "Just the casket, makeup, and delivery to the church and gravesite will be just fine," Herman said firmly.

"Dad, Grandma doesn't wear makeup," Josie said while tugging on her dad's hand, which Herman had clutched around Josie's ever since "Walter" has started staring at her.

Herman didn't reply. He only said, "Come along, Josie. I forgot her dress in the car." Josie had wiggled out of her dad's grip and was dawdling. She was curious about the elevator she had spotted in the rear of the showroom and thought maybe she could make another quick visit downstairs to see if anything strange had happened. "Hurry up, now," Herman said in an urgent, protective tone. She realized her stalling wouldn't work. Her father wasn't going leave her alone with Walter.

Outside, her father reached into the backseat of the state-issued sedan and unhooked the dress from the window handle. It was not a family secret that Josie's grandmother had an obsession with the color purple and not just any purple, but pastel lavender specifically. Her favorite lavender dress had purple violet blossoms on it and this was the one Herman was lifting out of the backseat for his mother's burial. Her favorite reclining-rocker chair always had a purple throw blanket draped over it. Josie couldn't remember her grandmother wearing anything other than purple. She even had purple polyester pants. Several times her grandmother mentioned that purple meant cosmic consciousness, or something like that about light. Josie didn't really understand, but she knew there were a lot of things in her grandparents' home that were purple, and they seemed to make her grandmother happy.

Her grandparents' bathroom had small floral-shaped purple soaps, which Josie was not supposed to use. But she never could resist, and she washed and washed her hands until the flower shape became a purple lathered orb. New ones would appear the next time she was over. However at some point her grandfather got wise to her soapy playtime and hid them, so Josie couldn't change their shape.

Josie liked purple but not to the point that all of her possessions needed to be the color of flowers. Nevertheless her mother, at her grandmother's request, had painted every surface of Josie's room purple. Josie wondered if since her grandmother was dead maybe now she could change the color. Should she keep it purple for the light thing? Her grandmother knew she was afraid of the dark, so maybe this was helping? Perhaps just one wall could be painted green. Josie loved green. Green grass, green leaves, and green caterpillars made her leap for joy. Bright kelly green was her favorite. Once she had seen a caterpillar that color in a book and was sure she'd find one outside someday.

When they returned home, Herman forgot to let Josie out of the backseat. His State Police car didn't have door handles inside either of the backseat doors. Herman did this frequently, to the point where his wife insisted that he get a new state car that didn't have the glass divider, since Josie got stuck once trying to crawl under the seats to get out through the front door. When her mother would realize Josie was missing, she always rushed out with an angry face, flung open the door with such force, and then hugged Josie very tight.

Recently Josie had learned to climb out through the front seat so easily that no one noticed she was locked in the back. She liked to think it was one of her many magic tricks. In case her father turned around and saw her exiting she opened and closed the back door. Not today though. She sat in the back and sobbed. Josie felt alone and couldn't stop crying. Her grandmother was her favorite person. Most people who knew her would say the same thing. She had an uncanny way of making everyone feel loved, though Josie received most of her special attention.

Josie knew her grandmother had possessed special powers, because she would tell Josie things before they happened. She'd say, "Watch this" as something silly, like someone dropping something, tripping or a dog running into a tree, would unfold. Sometimes it would be something scary, and she would tell Josie to close her eyes. Josie would hear a big crash and quickly open her eyes. One afternoon her grandfather was driving them to the shopping mall in downtown Flint and her grandmother firmly said, "Josie, close your eyes. Cover them now!"

There was a loud screech and a crash. Her grandfather was unable to hold back a yelp when he saw the bicyclist right in the middle of the car crash.

"Keep your eyes closed, Josie, until we turn the corner."

"A little more warning would be nice sometimes so I can pull over," her grandfather grumbled as his heart rate settled down.

"I knew we'd safely make the turn. I just didn't want Josie to see that."

"See what, Grandma? I'm getting older, you know."

"I know, Josie," she said, ignoring Josie's question.

Her grandmother was determined not to let fear enter her granddaughter's life. She continually scolded her son for bringing his work home, because Josie was a sensitive child who would be able to sense the violence. Josie especially worried about the important people in her life, and she was even known to fret about strangers. Deeply affected by the suffering of others, she tended to get caught up in what had happened and imagine possible outcomes and future scenarios. This was especially so concerning the crimes her father was working on. She mulled the meaning of life and death, and asked her father a never-ending list of questions about murder. There were times when Herman shrugged off Josie's questions, like when she asked, "Why do men murder more than women?" Other times Herman would go into great detail about blood loss and how the body works when she would ask questions about deadly gun wounds.

Herman's mother implored him, over and over, *not* to talk about his cases or any crime around Josie. Herman said that was all nonsense. He was a rationalist and only believed in things that could be proven by science. He assumed Josie loved science just like him and was nothing like his mother. His mother was said to have been a "sensitive child" when she was young. And his mother's psychic powers lost their charm on Herman when his twin brother died in a car crash. He believed his mother should have been able to stop his brother's death if she were truly gifted. He was her favorite son. It was after his brother's death that he changed his major in college from literature to science and soon after to forensics.

There was some confusion as to who was driving the car when his brother died since they were both ejected from the car. And Herman was in a comma for some time after the accident. So his mother demanded an investigation with both of their fingerprints plastered all over the steer wheel, since they shared the car, it was hard to tell who v driving even with forensics. So once Herman was in colle, he was determined to help advance the science of forensic so his mother would have no doubt that his brother wa driving that day.

After she had climbed out of the car without anyone noticing she was missing, Josie avoided her parents and went straight to her purple room. She stared at the midget-sized attic door in the corner of her bedroom, while her parents argued in their room about the funeral arrangements. Herman was complaining that he needed to work at the Lab today before the wake. Josie imagined silly circus clowns opening the attic door and inviting her saying, "Come along, through here you'll find laughter, no arguments."

Josie heard her father declare that he was going and wouldn't be too long. While listening closely by her bedroom door, she heard him heading for the backdoor. She remembered that she wanted to tell him about her dream about the case. It might help him be fast at the Lab, she thought. She rushed down the back stairs and out the screen door. There was a lip on the door threshold that she'd been warned about countless times not to trip. This time she did. She went flying, falling onto the driveway as the screen door hit her feet.

Herman returned exasperated from the garage and scolded her, "You know being careless gets you hurt. No one wins when you're careless. Look at you — you're bleeding. Now I'll have even less time at the Lab." Josie held her knee, which had a huge flap of skin peeled back. Blood gushed down her calf. She wanted to talk about blood evidence with her dad at that moment, but her mother rushed to the commotion and went into nurse mode, demanding, "We need to clean the wound, or it'll get infected. She may need stitches, look at this gash."

Herman interrupted, saying she would be just fine. "Just bandage her up. I need to get going."

As her mother sought first-aid supplies, Josie sat on the stairs and watched her father pull away in the car. The cat approached once Herman was gone and circled around her leg, licking the scrape. When her mother returned, she shooed the cat away saying that Tabby would give Josie Cat Scratch Fever. Josie said, "Doesn't she have to scratch me to do that?"

"I don't have time to tell you how disease works," Josie's mother said as she cleaned up the cut, adding hydrogen peroxide and not warning Josie it might hurt. But Josie had learned that the brown plastic bottle was something that caused pain and flinched before the bubbles even started foaming on her knee. "Now we have to choose a different dress for you to wear to the wake," her mother said as she put a huge Band-Aid on Josie's knee. Josie could tell her mother was upset and wanted to cheer her up, so she started singing, "I am stuck on Band-Aid brand 'cause Band-Aid's stuck on me!"

## The Wake

Josie wondered why it was called a wake. Was her grandmother possibly going to wake up like she did in the hospital? Was this wake intended to make sure the dead didn't wake up before you put them in the ground? Her grandmother was always talking about an awakening that might happen. Did that have something to do with a wake? Were other people supposed to wake up at this gathering? Her parents didn't seem in the mood to talk in the car, so Josie kept these questions to herself as they pulled into the funeral home parking lot.

Josie's mother had overdone the flowers for the wake and worried they might not look fresh for the funeral the

next day. Herman ignored her preoccupation with the flowers and left her fussing to greet the early arrivals. Soon the
room filled with family members and friends from Josie's
grandparents' church. Everyone looked terribly sad and
Josie felt overwhelmed by all the patting on the head and
apologies. It was as if these people had done something
wrong, since with each opening line started with "I'm sorry." Josie wanted to ask, "What did you do to her?" But she
had been urged to be on her best behavior, which to her
meant silence. Her house seemed the calmest when everyone was quiet — each person in his or her own individual
world. So Josie found simple things to focus on at the wake,
like shoes. First she started counting the number of brown
shoes, then women in heels versus flats. Her mother was
clear that you should never wear heels to a funeral because
you'd sink into the dirt at the burial site. It must be an eerie
sensation to be sinking alongside a lowering coffin, Josie
suspected. But Josie wondered if wearing heels to a wake
was okay, since everyone seemed to have extra high shoes
on. The feet, especially those belonging to old ladies, looked
swollen, bulging out of their pumps. Josie sat down on an
invitingly green loveseat to rest her own feet, which were
stuffed into her favorite pink ballet slippers. Sitting down
only increased the head patting, plus mothers and grandmothers then added, "You must be so tired, little Josie."

Josie was glad to be in the room with her grandmother
again until everyone filled up the space with all of their sad-
ness. The room became very heavy, and Josie felt tears well-

ing up. She wished people would start telling stories about the silly things that her grandmother used to do. Their repeated line, "It is such a tragedy that she left us so soon" wasn't making anyone feel better. It was moments like this when Josie wished she could tell a good joke or a funny story, but she was far too shy.

So she sat and remembered the time her grandmother put her elastic-waisted pants on backwards and didn't notice until they were all in the car. She had to wiggle out of them in the front seat while her grandfather yelled, "Hurry up, someone will see you. I told you women shouldn't wear pants. Skirts are much easier to twist around when you put them on wrong." Her grandmother giggled the whole time. She got her pants stuck on her shoes and had to take her shoes off. Then let out a huge laugh that filled the car when she saw that her underpants were on backwards too. "What on earth was happening when you were getting dressed?" Josie's grandfather asked.

"Oh, Josie and I were singing and dancing," her grandmother said in between laughing and finally getting dressed the right way around.

Recalling that time, Josie burst out laughing and the parlor room went still. Josie blushed as several people turned and looked at her with concern. A path through the crowd opened as though for royalty, and her mom appeared and sat down next to Josie.

"Sweet Josie, are you okay?" she said while rubbing off the smudged lipstick ladies had left all over Josie's cheek.

"Yeah, Mom. I was just remembering when grandma put her pants and underpants on backwards."

Her mother chuckled. "Well, we can't forget her ice cream cone joke." Josie laughed even louder. Her grandmother used to ask Josie if the ice cream smelled funny, smelling her own scoop and then looking at Josie to do the same. And when Josie went in for a smell, she would push her little nose into the soft serve and burst into a gigantic roar of a laugh. Josie believed she was getting wise to her grandmother's joke and she started ordering her ice cream dipped in hard chocolate — "a protective seal," Josie thought. But in one way or another, once Josie had gotten past the outer layer of chocolate, her grandmother would give her a little nudge or she'd pretend to stumble and run into Josie at just the right moment and Josie would always end up with ice cream on her nose.

"What about her singing the wrong words to "Over the Rainbow"? What was it she would mix up?" Josie asked.

Her mother laughed, "Bluebirds *die* and troubles melt like *gumdrops*."

Josie laughed and started to sing. The stuffy church members finally stopped frowning at all the laugher and joined in with Josie for the second verse. "Somewhere over the rainbow — Skies are blue — And the dreams that you dare to dream really do come true." Josie sang the next verse loudly changing lemon drops to gumdrops. She laughed again and stopped singing. The crowd had returned to chatter and softly her mother finished the song and hugged Josie.

Herman seemed happy when the mood in the room became somber again. He had never enjoyed his mother's silliness. It was more something that his brother shared with her. Herman had been a serious child and having a playful young daughter was a challenge to him and was bent on training her to be a great scientist. She loved her father's attention but was not always so interested in the science. Herman went into detail about how fingerprints were matched and how you could catch a thief with a print left behind on a doorknob or light switch. He taught Josie how to dust for prints around the house. Yet their trail of graphite powder on white walls infuriated Josie's mother. Josie generally listened dutifully to her father's teachings about forensics. Josie was more accepting of things science couldn't prove or at the very least was a naturalist and thought the pine tree in her backyard had big lessons to teach as many as her father. And while her father was teaching her the basics of the scientific process Josie usually had more questions about why the criminals did it, not how. Josie would ask, why do people steal? But she soon learned these weren't the theories her father wanted to discuss. There was something dark behind why men and women commit crimes that her father didn't know how to explain to Josie. He felt he was protecting her by only teaching her the "how to" of crime solving.

Josie wandered away from her mother and stood beside her father, who was surrounded by his coworkers. Most of the family members had gone home to prepare the meal for the funeral luncheon at Josie's house the following day. The meal was most likely to be similar to what had started filling their refrigerator since her grandmother's death. Josie wasn't sure who was going to eat all the casseroles, which all tasted like cream of mushroom soup, no matter what combination of meats, frozen vegetables, noodles, or rice were added. In the past few days, she had consumed enough casserole for a lifetime. However, the Tupperware filled with cookies and cakes spanning the countertop overjoyed Josie, since her mother rarely let her eat sweets.

Josie thought back to the time a friend bought her one of those candy "jewel" rings. The purple jewel on her ring finger delighted Josie and she flashed a prideful smile towards her friend as she turned to head home. Making sure it was gone before she entered the backdoor, she rapidly licked that sugar ring down to the plastic holder. But when she looked in the mirror, she gasped — her lips and whole mouth were purple. Panicked, she washed her own mouth out with soap hoping to get rid of the purple. No luck. She wasn't able to hide the candy's trace. She had to face her mother in shame, who predictably scolded her, reminding her that grandmother had diabetes and sugar was what probably caused her cancer. But there was an exception to the rule, the holidays. With all the family around and everyone off work, the funeral was beginning to feel like one.

———

Smoke had started to fill the parlor room pretty heavily at this point and Josie looked around for half-smoked cigarettes in the ashtrays. Since her dream with the cigarette smell, she had started collecting used cigarettes and hiding them in her room. Her father collected all sorts of things. In his home lab he had a large collection of rocks, fibers, fur, hair, knives, trowels, and dirt from all over the world. She wasn't sure what she would do with the butts. It was at least a tangible thing she could collect from her dream, since her mother said no to the rabbit idea. Even though the Lab guys on the police radio said the cigarette butt didn't seem significant to the case, Josie couldn't help but wonder about a possible connection. Her grandmother was always talking about how everything was connected. Moreover, the stale smell of cigarette butts helped her remember the details of her dream, which she was trying to keep them fresh until her father had time to listen.

# 3

## Rust Investigation

While the Banks family was taking time off after the funeral, the Rust murder investigation was turned over to the local detectives. Josie listened through the air vent when her father secretly called work to hear about the case. The detectives told Herman that they discovered the young victim had been out for a walk with her pet rabbit at the time of the murder. According to the victim's mother, the girl walked the rabbit nearly everyday. When Herman heard this he thought about Josie walking her cat and felt a twinge of fear and anger that this little girl could have been his own. Herman brushed off the comparison, though; remembering that this girl was much older and the victim's mother had said her daughter had a boyfriend. Herman assumed the girl's rabbit walking was an excuse to see her boyfriend, and Josie was way too young for boyfriends. He still didn't think the rabbit was essential to solving the case.

Later, the detectives questioned the boyfriend. Rabbit hairs were all over his dirty clothes tucked in the back of his closet convincing the detectives he was part of the crime.

The teenager claimed that he saw the victim and her rabbit every day. He pleaded that there was rabbit hair on everything he owned. It was the muddy shoes the officers found in his closet that earned him his handcuffs.

This small town case didn't go away fast enough for the locals. The suspect was jailed and his father aggressively protested for his release. He called a neighboring county judge at home and parked himself in front of the local jail flapping unsigned judge's release orders hoping to get more attention to set his son free. Problems with the evidence seemed to keep popping up. The forensic clothing footprint match became controversial. With the boyfriend in custody, it should have been a quickly closed case, but the shoe prints were still in question. It was rare to find a footprint on fabric, but the nature of the nylon held the soil in place in its weave. Herman was advocating for the evidence's validity. The issue of evidence reliability led the Bridgeport Regional Laboratory to present this case to a monthly unit technical conference. The normally dull government meeting was heated, as several older scientists didn't agree with Herman's findings. However they did agree that the Unit Board would re-photograph the jacket to make a *better* comparison. Herman inwardly berated the Board with vulgar disagreements throughout the meeting, but he didn't dare say anything.

The Board's findings were that it was *not* a forensic match. So the other forensic scientists in the state sided against Herman and the Bridgeport Regional Laboratory team, which forced the evidence to then be ruled inconclusive. The Board said Herman had made a mistake and such a finding would hurt the prosecutor's case. The boyfriend was set free. Herman, enraged, went home and smashed some beakers, tossing around all sorts of containers of collected samples and papers in his home lab. Positioned flat on the floor in the corner of her bedroom, Josie listened closely through the air vent. There were several loud crashes, glass breaking, and vulgar cursing that Josie had never heard her father say before. The noise settled down, and her dad called up the stairs for her. Herman was determined to prove them wrong and needed Josie's help to do so.

First, he used one of Josie's nylon jackets and had Josie step in dirt and then step on the jacket in several different pairs of sneakers, including her mom's that were twice as big as Josie's feet. They used all different kinds of dirt, which he had Josie gather from the backyard. "Make sure you dig deep so the soil is damp," her father yelled at her as she went out the backdoor with a small shovel and several little kitchen bowls — bowls that Josie's mom would later toss out in a huff, saying they were now too unsanitary to use.

As Josie dug, she recalled that her grandfather had once said she could reach China if she kept digging deep enough. The kids at school had laughed at her when she repeated his story. Once Josie learned about the earth's core, how hot it was, and how there was no way to get through to China. She couldn't understand why her grandfather didn't know that. After all, he was a school principal.

While Josie stood in her mother's shoes, she asked her dad if they could get a bunny. Herman had a quizzical look on his face and firmly said no. Josie hopped away in the big shoes when her dad said they were done. Herman laughed and said, "Be careful, you may tip over." Just then she did — landed nose first in the grass and laughed a contagious roar of joy that even Herman, in his foul mood, couldn't hold back a chuckle.

Herman's findings from using Josie's coat confirmed the teenage victim's evidence. With single-minded focus, ignoring his wife's requests to eat something, Herman wrote a report that ended up being ninety pages long and presented it at the next Forensics National Conference. In the meantime, the Bridgeport Regional Laboratory decided to have an outside consultant, Herman's retired professor from Michigan State University, evaluate the evidence. To prepare the evidence for the new testing the Lab re-photographed the victim's jacket, and Herman found even more matching points, all the identifying marks.

The professor's findings confirmed Herman's. It was a match. The Board reviewed the case again and the boyfriend was officially charged. With all of this deliberation back and forth, the prosecutor decided to plea-bargain rather than go to trial. When the Lab secretary relayed the news to Herman he slammed his fist on the desk at work. Soon after Herman's outburst he was called in to a meeting with the Lieutenant, Herman's immediate supervisor. Herman talked so fast about why the plea was an injustice that his boss told him to slow down. Finally, he took a breath, listened and then reluctantly agreed with the Lieutenant and prosecutor that it was in the best interest to not air this controversy out in court. It would be too technical to convince a jury. So the boyfriend agreed to plead guilty to second-degree murder *with* the possibility of parole.

No one even cared about the rabbit hairs on the boyfriend's clothes at that point. Herman believed that with the hair, fiber traces, and prints it was a closed case. Despite his frustration, he was convinced the boyfriend deserved the electric chair.

Although Josie never heard the results of her traipsing in dirt in her mother's shoes, she assumed it solved the case somehow by her dad's change in mood. He was home more for dinner, even praising Martha's cooking. Josie was happy that she had played a small part in this closed case.

# 4

Flash! Bang! There were three loud bangs and three blinding flashes of light in a pitch-dark room. Josie forced her eyes open before she saw more. "Gunshots! Gunshots!" she screamed. The phone rang and her dad hurried downstairs as her mom leapt out of bed and ran down the hall to Josie's room. "It's just the phone ringing, honey. There were no gunshots. Go back to sleep. It's the middle of the night." Josie's mom climbed into bed next to her and tried to comfort her. "It's just a dream, honey. Try to go back to sleep." Martha played with Josie's hair until she was sure she had fallen back asleep. Josie had recently learned how to fake sleeping just to get her mom out of the room, so she could make little drawings about her dreams.

Josie heard her dad come back upstairs after the phone call. He swiftly shuffled around, preparing to leave. After slowly slipping out of the bed, Josie's mom left the room. Seconds later, Josie pulled out her paper and markers.

"Someone was shot and killed in Owosso," Herman said as he put on his work clothes including his bulky rubber boots. "There were gunshots. Maybe what my mother said to her meant something." Josie heard her father say from across the hall. She wanted to hear more so she crawled out of bed and listened by her door.

"That's silly. The phone ringing startled her," Josie's mom said in a fearful tone.

"She screamed before the phone rang," Herman said in his investigative work tone.

"She screamed before *we* heard the phone ring," Martha said as though trying to convince herself. She knew Herman would argue differently no matter what she said. Since Herman's mother died they disagreed about nearly everything, including simple things like what toppings should they get on the pizza or what temperature the thermostat should be set on.

After her father left that morning, Josie stumbled sleepily down the hall towards her parent's room, and then Martha tucked her into their bed, though she disliked Josie sleeping in her bed. And it was rare that she was even allowed in their room. But as Josie slept on her father's pillow in peace, her mother thought maybe the exile needed to come to an end. Though Josie was clearly too old for such privileges, it was important she was rested so as not to fall behind in the third grade. Martha paced and cleaned while Josie slipped into a deep sleep. She was visibly upset that her husband's work was distressing her daughter.

Once asleep Josie began to dream again. As Martha watched her rapid eye movements, she wondered if Josie was really having psychic dreams. And as Josie's began to thrash a bit in her sleep, Martha thought maybe she should wake her up. She waited, impatiently, biting at her cuticles, to see if it would pass.

Josie was dreaming about shopping for groceries at a store she had never been in before. Frantically she had searched for her mom in the aisles, but didn't see anyone she knew. Not finding her anywhere, she went out to the parking lot to look for her mom's car, and as she wandered down the first row a man grabbed her from behind. She was too afraid to turn around to look to see who it was. Josie's eyes flew open, and she looked frightened.

Her mom quickly sat down close and clutched Josie's shoulders, "Honey, what did you see?"

"I couldn't see him. He grabbed me. He took me away," Josie said in a panic.

"It's okay Josie." Martha said while she patted Josie's shoulders. "You don't have to remember anything. Just try and rest."

"But I want to remember. I want to help Dad solve the murder." Josie sat up.

"Honey, your dreams have nothing to do with his job." Her mom gently nudged her to lie back down.

"But didn't he say someone was shot?"

"How did you hear that?" Her mom stood up and hovered over the side of the bed.

"They were, weren't they? Someone was shot in my dream. I heard three shots," Josie said with conviction.

"Oh Josie, it was just a dream, and your mind tricks you."

"No, I heard three, with three flashes of light. Was a woman shot three times?"

"They're just dreams, Honey. We all dream things when we sleep. They're not real. We'll look up what dreams mean in the Encyclopedia Britannica when you get up." Her mom tucked her tightly under the covers.

"But what about what Grandma said?"

"She was on a lot of medicine when she said that. We can't know that it meant anything. Please try to get some rest — it's so early."

## Owosso Crime Scene

A local Owosso farmer was checking his squirrel traps under the white pines close to his home when he stumbled upon a nearly nude woman's body. All the farmer saw, and what the local police said on the phone to Operations, and then relayed to Herman, was that she was shot multiple times. It turned out to be the body of Lorraine Babb who had disappeared during her routine shopping trip to town a few weeks back. She had bought clothes and groceries for her husband and one-year-old son and then apparently walked to her truck in the strip-mall parking lot and never seen again until the farmer found her dead amongst the leaves and pine needles.

The morning after her disappearance her father-in-law found her truck sitting alone in the parking lot with the door wide open, groceries on the front seat, and her keys lying on the ground near the vehicle. He was outraged no one else had noticed the door ajar, which was visible from the road.

For two days, nearly 4,000 volunteers had helped search for her. Shiawassee County Deputy Till Zimmerman recalled that a line of people walked the entire county from M-21 north to Sleepy Hollow State Park. The volunteers were spread 100 feet apart, like a horizontal marching band. They canvassed the cornfields and woods but found no trace of Lorraine. Some of the volunteers were convinced that they had searched the area where she was later found. However, according to the sheriff's office, the search stopped about a half mile short of where the farmer found her body.

When Herman arrived on the scene, he confirmed she had been shot three times, once in the back and twice in the head. The autopsy would have to confirm the order of each shot, but Herman was pretty convinced the one in the back had come first. She must have been trying to get away, he thought. He also noted evidence that she had been raped. The bullet in the back led him to wonder if the rape was after she was killed and dumped in the woods. It also appeared that semen would likely be recovered. The rape looked recent, but her injuries looked older. Suspiciously, he then wondered if the farmer had actually gotten *his* kicks before calling the police. With a crinkled brow Herman watched him closely for a few minutes. The man was old and visibly shaking. Not the killing type, Herman thought.

"Not a pro," Herman mumbled and told the officers they were looking for someone who knew her. It was probably a crime of passion or a kid who was losing control and could quickly turn into a serial killer.

"A kid?" one young local cop said.

"Well a young man, since obviously he's past puberty," Herman said as he held up a small sample bag of semen he had collected when it fell out of the victim, dripping down her leg, as they rolled her over.

"Wow. All of that came out of her just from when we rolled her over?" asked the same quizzical cop.

"We're lucky it didn't get lost. Normal procedure would have been to extract this at autopsy."

"How do you test that to make sure it's semen?" asked the young cop, who was staying close by Herman since he arrived.

"You looking to go into forensics someday, kid?" Herman asked in a fatherly tone.

"Yeah, it looks interesting," the officer said with raised eyebrows with a thrilled tone in his voice.

"Okay, here's what you do. You need to test a fabric stain or actual seminal fluid — in this case we actually have a large sample of fluid. Either way we are looking for the presence of acid phosphatase, an enzyme that is present in high levels in seminal fluid. We take a small sample or swab from this," Herman held up the bag labeled 'Crime Scene Extracted Vaginal Fluid.' In his other hand was a bag labeled 'Victim's Underpants' which were tossed at the scene, looking almost staged. "We test it using a presumptive screening test. A color change from clear to a purple color is considered to be a positive reaction."

"Oh and that's it," the young cop said with confidence. He also hoped it was the end of the lecture so he could get back to his supervisor.

"Well, no. The presence of semen is confirmed by a microscopic identification of spermatozoa in a stain. Most labs use a chemical staining process or what we call a Christmas Tree Stain to enable the sperm to be seen among all the other cells and bacteria present in the sample."

"Christmas Tree Stain. I can remember that one." The young cop appeared to follow what Herman was talking about. But he looked over his shoulder concerned his supervisor could be looking for him.

"Now the individual sperm heads can also be accurately identified based on their morphological characteristics, using a phase contrast. An ideal, mature spermatozoon has an oval shaped head with a regular contour with a pale anterior part and a darker posterior region."

As Herman went on and on, the young cop's brow crinkled up. He was nodding frequently unrelated to Herman's explanation. Herman kept talking and not noticing that the kid was starting to look bewildered. "If no spermatozoa are located, such as from people with vasectomies, an extract can be tested to identify the presence of the human prostate specific protein called p30. With no one to match fluid to, the case goes cold. Let's hope we can find someone to match. Maybe someone was recently released with a rape record."

"Not sure there are many of those around here," the cop said to break up Herman's steady stream of science facts.

"Everyone's ego can be pushed to the point of murder," Herman said. "However rape adds a whole other dimension to this crime. Plus you'd be surprised who lives next door."

## Sparrow Street

Josie woke up in her parents' bed, with a note on the pillow next to her. "Sweet Josie, I hope you got some rest. I was called into work. Please go next door when you get up and Aunt Caroline will fix you something to eat. Love, Mom."

Although Josie had no intention of going next door. There was work to be done. She went to her room with Tabby on her heels and pulled out her notebooks. With her favorite pen, she drew a room with a long shaft of light shining into the corner. In her recent dream there had been a naked, young woman who was curled up like a cat. She didn't appear to be sleeping, but rather, shaking. Josie wondered how to draw someone shaking. She didn't try, but watched Tabby sleep and drew her instead in the corner of the dark room. There was a shadow covering up something else in the corner that Josie couldn't see. She saw the shadow was shaped like a man and felt a chill. Was it the man who grabbed her in her dream? She wanted to stop drawing, but she heard her grandmother's voice saying, "Mind your dreams." Josie was beginning to take that phrase as an order, as if they were the only things she needed to pay attention to. She sat still and let the whole dream flow over her again, beginning with the three flashes. She couldn't wait to find out from her dad if there were three bullets. Restless, she ran downstairs, called her dad's work and asked to be put through to him on the radio.

"Josie, we can't do that," said the Lab secretary, a woman who Josie wasn't convinced was a woman. She had met her several times on her visits to the Lab. She was the gatekeeper. When an officer or other state employee had a bag of evidence in hand to submit or to discuss a case with the appropriate scientist, she had to let them in the locked door that prevented their entry and free movement around the laboratory. She also held the special key to another locked door that protected the evidence in a small room to the left that Josie had only been in a few times. She never gave access to unfamiliar visitor — for them there were evidence lockers, like small school lockers, located in the lobby in case the appropriate scientist was not available (maybe on vacation or in court). The visitor could then place the evidence in the locker, slam the door, and only the scientist assigned to it could open it later to retrieve the evidence. In that way, the chain of custody is intact and as short as possible. Though Josie was always let through the door with her father, Josie was struck how the secretary's voice was hard and firm like the male cops and she didn't give hugs.

"But it's important." Josie tried to use a grownup voice and not sound like a little girl begging — like the kids she sometimes overheard at the mall, pleading to their moms for the latest or coolest toy.

"Is your mother okay?" The secretary was trying to figure out how important it was.

"Yeah, she's at work."

"Are you all alone?" The secretary now sounded concerned.

Josie looked at Tabby. "No." She figured it wasn't a lie. Though Tabby was not a person, her cat was certainly more capable of companionship than her aunt. Josie's Aunt Caroline was a basket of nerves and had her hands full with her own kids. Josie didn't get along with her cousins very well. They treated her like a stepsister, the middle child since Josie's birthday landed right between theirs. Besides they fought with each other all the time and there was enough fighting in her house. She didn't need to be around other people arguing too.

"Josie, you still there?"

"Yes, I need to ask him a question. Can you just ask it for me and then let me know what he says?"

"Sure, though they may not be near their car radios. But I'll try. What's the question?"

"Was the woman shot three times?"

"Oh, Josie. You, well, don't need to know that." The secretary seemed flustered by the unexpected matter-of-factness in Josie's tone.

"Yes, I do. I need to know if my dream was right, so I can finish this drawing for him, so he can catch the killer."

"Josie, maybe you can try working on another drawing. Maybe something pretty that I can post at my desk. Like some pine trees you did on last year's Christmas cards. I heard that you are quite the artist."

"I can do that too. But this dream with a dark room and three flashes of light just won't stop replaying. If I get it down on paper sometimes it makes it stop going over and over in my mind." Josie said this anxiously, which seemed to concern the secretary. She then quickly responded, "Okay. I'll see what I can do. Hold on."

Josie could hear her calling on the CB. Josie tried to remember her father's CB number, so that if she had to call again, maybe she could just do it from the police scanner and radio in the den. Josie had written down all the police codes she had heard over the years. She knew that a 901 was a murder, 1300 was an assault, 1206 meant an armed robbery. She also had gotten into trouble in school when she used Ten Codes, police radio codes, in her English assignment instead of proper salutations.

After several attempts she heard the woman say, "Your daughter is on the line. I told her I'd ask you a question for her." Straining to hear, Josie couldn't make out her father's garbled response and wondered if the secretary could. "Yes, she's at home and seems a little upset and concerned about the case you're on."

"What's the question?" Josie heard her father say sternly.

"She wants to know if the woman was shot three times."

"Tell her yes," Herman said.

"But sir, how did she know that?"

"She must have overheard me on the phone this morning."

"But…"

Herman cut her off. "Tell Josie I'll be home for dinner and not to worry so much."

"Okay, I will. Good luck with the investigation."

"Thanks. I should be back in the Lab in a few hours."

"Josie, your dad said yes."

"Thanks," Josie hung up and didn't even say goodbye. She flew up the stairs to start drawing again.

"Josie, you still there?" The Lab secretary sighed and noisily placed the receiver back on the handset cradle.

———

Herman searched for footprints, but each one near the body looked fresh from the trooper's boots. She must have been dumped on a dry day, maybe yesterday, Herman thought. They finished up collecting soil samples and maggots on the ground from where the body was discarded as the coroner put her body in the van.

While tailgating the van, with his Lab partners consistently commenting that he was too close, Herman thought about why the killer redressed half of her. There were signs that she had been completely nude at one point. She was dirty under her clothes with smudges like soot and scrapes as if she had been on a cement slab. She wasn't killed in the woods. There was no pools of blood or sign of struggle — the leaves were barely rustled. And her palms or fingernails weren't covered in mud. Why such a public dumping so close to where she was taken? Definitely it's someone who thinks they're smart and will get away with it. Maybe they even planted the semen. Maybe it's someone who's just fucking with me.

"So Herman, what was that all about with Josie?" John from the Lab asked while fiddling with radio channels trying to see if they were in range for channel 2. He was about to call in to let them know they had time-sensitive evidence that needed to be processed by another forensic team because they were most likely going to be sent home for too many overtime hours.

"Oh, nothing much. She's been having nightmares ever since her grandmother died. I'm sure they'll pass soon."

"But we didn't know how many shots — the local police didn't have a clue, so she just guessed three? What about your own mother, wasn't she psychic?"

"John, I don't want my daughter treated like a psychic freak. She just made a lucky guess. She has no special powers. She's just a smart, little girl who loves science," Herman barked.

"Okay, I understand." John looked out the window and left Herman alone the rest of the way back to the Lab.

Herman didn't want his daughter treated like his mother when she was a kid. However Herman had only heard stories, it sounded like she was made to perform like some freak of nature — guessing people's futures and surprising people with details of their past. The police department relentlessly consulted her on unsolved cases when she was a young mother. Herman vaguely remembered going to the police station and sitting with his mother in one of those small interrogation rooms while she drew out sketches. He was given crayons and paper too, but lacked any sort of creative talent.

———

At home, Josie was pacing back and forth and thinking about how she never had a chance to tell her father about her dream with the rabbit and little girl. Which was why she figured if she did a painting about the current case, her father would see it and ask her about it. He was a visual person, always reading or looking at something. He didn't talk much at home and the silence seemed thicker since his mother had died. Josie was told to be quiet more often and her mother spent more hours at work or in bed right after dinner.

Josie wanted to paint all three scenes: The truck parked at the grocery store, the bare room where the woman was held, and the shooting. First, she needed to find her old toy truck for a model. She cracked open the small door in her room that led to the attic. She reached for the long string dangling down from the bulb hanging on the ceiling way up in the rafters. If you brushed it and didn't get in on the first grab, it swung spastically and then it would be nearly impossible for Josie to grab even on her tiptoes. Thankfully, this time she caught it on the first try. The light illuminated a cluttered mess of old toys, a bucket of Petoskey stones, opened boxes of her grandmother's clothes, bags of baby clothes (even though she had overheard her parents crying about not being able to get pregnant again) and a mound of dolls whose faces her mother thought were too real and might be causing her nightmares. Josie stood on the middle step and quickly scanned the room for the red truck. "There it is!" She ran up the stairs grabbed it like a relay baton and ran back down the stairs, leaping for the light string and tugging. She slammed the little door and took a deep breath. Then she sat down with her paints and drew a perfect rendition of her toy red truck and the outside of her local grocery store. It wasn't the one in the dream but she had a better memory of her local Kroger.

That night Herman walked past the paintings, which were taped to the fridge when he arrived home. After her dad didn't notice them, she moved the one with the dark room with flashes of light onto the counter where her father set his leftovers.

"What's this, Josie?" Herman asked glancing down while unwrapping his dinner.

"It's why I called you at work. I needed to know for sure how many shots, so I could finish the painting."

"Is this cement or dirt?" Herman pointed to the floor.

"Cement. Maybe even wet cement but I didn't know how to paint the difference."

"Where is this?" Herman asked and looked at Josie for the first time since he arrived home.

"I don't know." Josie shrugged and lowered her eyes.

"Can you see the outside of this room in your dream?" Herman asked and pointed to the door in the painting.

"I don't think so, just the inside and a sliver through the door maybe, but the man is standing in the way."

Pressing the issue, Herman asked, "What do you see outside the door?"

"I don't think I can see anything."

"Can you try?" Herman was surprised how life-like her painting was. It looked like a crime scene photo. Still he had always been suspicious of his mother's psychic gift, he realized this might help him quickly solve the case.

"Okay, let me sit and close my eyes. Since I already drew it, it may be gone."

"What do you mean, gone?"

"The dreams fade after I draw them. It's like, well…"

"Okay, I understand." After cutting Josie off, Herman directed her towards a chair. "Close your eyes, and tell me what you see."

Josie sat still at the dining room table, propped up like a doll in a big chair. She squinted her eyes tight and then she waited. She tried to look around in her mind but everything was blank, dark. "I'm scared. I can't see anything. Daddy, I want to help, but…"

"Josie, it's okay," Herman said. Josie quickly opened her eyes, her pupils full and dark as night. "This painting helps," he said. "Can I keep this one?"

"Of course!" Josie squeezed her dad's legs, and she was thrilled to be helping with the case.

"Now, it's getting late. You go get ready for bed," Herman said as he untangled himself from Josie's arms.

Josie went upstairs with Tabby cradled in her arms. She brushed her teeth, with her cat reluctantly tucked under one arm, squirming each time Josie turned on the water. She softly said goodnight to her mom, who was already in bed with a headache.

"Josie, I forgot," she mumbled and scooted up against the headboard. "I bought you something to use in your room. It's over there by my purse. Can you bring that bag here?"

Josie wanted to immediately look in, but brought the bag to her mom as she was instructed.

Josie's mom pulled out a large, silver flashlight and a pack of two D batteries.

Josie's eyes widened. "Is that for me?" The flashlight was so heavy Josie wondered if her mom was giving it to her for protection, like the club her dad had under his side of the bed.

"You can keep it by your bed and use it to light up your room. You can shine light on your dreams when they're too scary," her mom said softly.

Josie had grown increasingly afraid of the dark since the crime scene dreams started. Nightly she chanted several lines from her favorite Shel Silverstein's poem:

"I'm Reginald Clark, I'm afraid of the dark — So I always insist on the light on, …I'm Reginald Clark, I'm afraid of the dark — So please do not close this book on me."

When she was really little she would only sleep if the bedroom overhead light was left on. Later it was okay if only the hallway light was on with the door wide open, and then the door only had to be open a crack. Then finally the hall light could be turned off. Herman continually complained about having to buy new light bulbs. Josie had now regressed back to needing the hall light on and the door wide open. Her mom was hoping the flashlight would help make the process go faster this time.

"Thank you, Mom," Josie said while hugging her mom. Her mom was such a light sleeper she seemed to know each time Josie flicked on the light switch. Now she could secretly draw under the covers and not have to turn on the light. And I can sneak downstairs every once in awhile for the hidden cookies like Dad does in the dark, Josie thought.

## The Ruger

A few days later a local Owosso teenage boy was fishing in a river close to his home when he stepped on the barrel of a .22-caliber revolver. The local Owosso police called the Bridgeport Regional Laboratory and Herman drove up alone to the site where the gun was found. It puzzled Herman why criminals would ever dump a weapon near . Why not take the time to dispose of it later? He maybe this kid is local and under suspicion for something and needed to get rid of it fast. Maybe his dad is a cop, or maybe he's just dumb. Dumb is more like it. Herman began plotting how to outsmart his own investigation team and quickly solve this case without having to tell them about Josie's drawings, and he was actively seeking a promotion after the fabric footprint drew some national attention. And he was pretty convinced this woman's murder would be solved because of how the evidence was lining up.

Once Herman arrived, with the local police, he combed the bank of the river. On the opposite side of the riverbank from the gun, Herman found the victim's wallet containing a photo ID. "We are lucky this water hasn't frozen yet or this young man wouldn't be out fishing," one of the local cops said, while he grabbed the boy's shoulder. Herman took a good look at the boy. Why was he fishing? It was damn cold out. He wouldn't plant this just to see if he could throw us off, would he? Herman closely watched him chat with the officers. Nope. No vestige of puberty yet. His voice was higher than Martha's and he lacked facial hair.

"Yeah, who knows what this wallet would look like by spring," Herman said after an awkward delay. Herman wasn't sure he believed in luck though. There had to be a logical reason for everything. 'This causes that' was Herman's way of thinking. He firmly believed in the scientific method. He depended on causation. His criminology professors instructed him to be prepared for all circumstances, one step ahead of the mind of a murderer. Herman took this as a mantra for his life. Always planning the smallest detail of any event. This was how also Herman accounted for why he had bought his new insulated rubber boots just days ago. Without the boots, he wouldn't have been able to cross the river and find the wallet. His mother would have called that Divine intervention, but not Herman — it was his preparedness that was key to finding solutions. He wanted to reject Josie's dreams, but he felt there were such strong links to reality that he couldn't ignore.

Back at the Lab, Herman compared the slugs pulled from Lorraine's body to slugs he test fired with the recovered .22-caliber revolver. The normal wear and tear from use caused the firearm to create distinct characteristics over time, which was found on the bullets in Lorraine's body and the test-fired slugs. Herman's report concluded that the gun they found was the murder weapon.

## Sparrow Street

"So I found a match with the gun I found in the river. And got to use the water tank in the Lab garage."

"The what?"

"A bullet recovery tank used to test fire guns. The bullets safely fall to the bottom of the tank and are recovered with a long stick with a little gum on the end. The test bullet is than compared on the comparison microscope with bullets recovered from the victim or crime scene."

"Oh. Which case is that again?"

"The one with three gunshots that Josie dreamt about."

"You didn't show her the gun did you?" Martha stopped washing the dishes and looked over her shoulder at Herman pacing in the kitchen.

"No, this isn't about Josie."

"Oh, okay. I'm sorry, please continue."

"So they finally traced the gun to the original known owner. But the trace was more like a scavenger hunt. The search started with the State Police sending all the information they had about the gun — including the manufacturer and model — to an office worker in a low-slung brick building off the Appalachian Trial in rural West Virginia, about ninety miles northwest of Washington. I had to go there once."

"I remember that."

"Well, then it was the job of the ATF officials to call the manufacturer, who revealed which wholesaler the company used. This lead them to call a second distributor before investigators could pinpoint the retail gun dealer who initially sold the weapon. Gun dealers are required to keep a copy of federal forms that indicates which dealer buys which gun as well as to log all guns sold. They are required to divulge that information to the ATF if a gun is found at a crime scene, and the authorities want it traced. Often and in this case, the gun shops fax the paperwork to the ATF."

"Uh-huh." Martha said as she swirled a towel around a frying pan, patting it dry.

"In about thirty percent of cases, one or all of the gun shops have gone out of business. ATF tracers then sort through potentially thousands of out-of-business records forwarded to the ATF and stored at an office building resembling a remote call center more than a law enforcement operation."

"Have you been there too?" Martha said trying to pretend she was still interested.

Herman paused then went on without answering her question, "The tracing center receives about a million out-of-business records every month. A private company runs the center's sorting and imaging operations from six a.m. to midnight, five days a week. Two shifts of contracted workers spend their days taking staples out of papers, sorting through thousands of pages, and taking pictures of the records. The images are stored on old-fashioned microfilm reels. There's no way to search the records, other than to scroll through the reel one page at a time. Luckily there was no searching in this case. But it still was a laborious paper trail requiring way too many hours on the phone for me. You know how I hate to be on the phone."

Martha nodded her head in affirmation.

"After all that, they discovered one James Goodwin who had bought it at a pawnshop in Yuma, Arizona. But they had no other information on James Goodwin. He was nearly impossible to track. Even with the stack of papers they received from the DMV with a dozen other people named James Goodwin. The case went cold. There was no semen match either."

"I'm sorry, Herman." Martha was worried how frustrated Herman seemed to be.

"We need an eyewitness to the kidnapping." Josie's dream popped into Herman's mind. Maybe he could get her to remember what the kidnapper looked like. Without a word Herman left Martha in the kitchen with a never-ending pile of dishes and went upstairs to find Josie, but she was already asleep.

The following day Herman went home, while his wife was still at work, and asked Josie a series of questions. Based on her answers, he had some indication of height, weight, and hair color, but facial features were tough for her to remember. "I know I've never seen him before," Josie said.

"Do you remember everyone you see?" he asked.

"Yes, don't you?"

"No, Josie. Hmm... let me think of a stranger we met recently. Oh, can you tell me what the guy looked like who pumped our gas last weekend?"

"Tall skinny man, looked like he was a farmer — a bit out of place at a city gas station. He had light brown hair like mine, a little longer than yours but not like a hippie, a big smile with some crooked teeth. That's why I thought he was a farmer. His eyes were light blue and smiled. I think he had a bigger nose, but not like our cousins, just long and narrow. His name on his overalls said Frank. But he didn't look like a Frank and they were too big for him, so I think he was borrowing someone else's overalls."

Herman could barely remember even looking at the man, so it may have been a poor question because he couldn't confirm her facts. The details sounded accurate and he was astounded by how much she remembered. He knew all too well that most eyewitnesses were only right fifty percent of the time. He wondered if Josie had a photographic memory and thought he should have her tested for that. "Thanks, Josie. You've been a big help. Let's keep this conversation between us. We don't want to worry your mom. Okay?"

"Okay, I understand. Have I been causing her headaches?"

"No, no. She's been working too much. The hospital is stressful."

"Okay, I'm going to take Tabby for a walk until Mom gets home to make dinner."

"Okay, be safe."

"I will." Josie wondered what could be unsafe about a walk around the block. Her neighborhood was lovely with small groves of pine trees, parks, and a barn at the end of the road. All of her dad's cases happened far away. She couldn't imagine something happening around here and her grandmother said she would be safe here and not to worry about crime. Tabby followed closely behind Josie on the sidewalk. Her mother had started walking Tabby when she was just a kitten. At first her mother had used a leash. Now Tabby never strayed unless the birds, which seemed to always hover close by, swooped down to dive bomb. Then Tabby would give chase — this usually happened in the spring when the blue jays were nesting.

Josie used to think the birds were following Tabby, but later she noticed when she walked home from school alone that sparrows would fly in front of her and hop along the sidewalk. When she got too close they would fly off and circle back in front of her. Of course it wasn't until the crows started regularly coming around and her grandmother made note of it that anyone believed Josie had wild birds as friends. Josie was close to getting one of the crows to take crackers from her hand.

One time, Josie carried a dead baby blue jay in her pocket for a few days. Then her mother noticed a stain forming on her pants pocket. They were cream-colored pants, and Josie was surprised it took her so long to notice. First, her mom was just upset that Josie had a stained her pants, but then, when she found the bird, her mom jumped with fright and blamed Herman for talking about dead things so much. That was when she told Herman that Josie could no longer visit the crime Lab on Sundays, which had been their normal Sunday routine, kind of like church, since Josie was four. There was that time when Josie spattered-painted her pants red like the bloodstained jeans she saw at the Lab in the stink room, a room behind a locked door in the garage. That particular Sunday the ventilated room was full of bloody clothing taken off dead bodies, now dry and stiff. Martha was not pleased with the painted pants she created but still didn't cut off the visits to the Lab at that point — now the dead bird was just too much.

Her mother pulled into the driveway as Josie was just about to beat her own jump rope record. She was trying to sing the song — "Blackbirds. Blackbirds. Sitting on a wire. What do you do there? May we inquire? Oh we just sit to see the day. Then we flock and fly away. By one, two, three." — ten times while jumping rope, which would have been her record. She was just shy of ten when her mom's car turned in, blinding Josie with the headlights, and Martha slammed on the brakes. Josie thought her mom was going to be mad. Instead her mom quickly got of the car and she said, "I'm sorry. I didn't mean to scare you. I'm so happy to see you out playing."

# 5

A few weeks later after Josie had been spending most of her free time drawing crime scenes for her father, she woke up and noticed that her cat was missing from the bed. It was early, still dark, hours before her mother would wake her for school, Josie knew her parents were sound asleep, both had a habit of taking sleeping pills, so she tiptoed out of her room to find out where Tabby had gone. She searched the kitchen first and then all around the first floor in Tabby's normal hiding places — behind the thick green curtains by the heating vent on the floor — on top of the La-Z-Boy's armrest tucked in a corner of the dark den — the window-seat cushion in the stuffy sitting room. Then she looked in the basement by the litter box where Tabby sometimes sat when she wasn't feeling well. No luck. She headed back up to the second floor and searched her room. Sometimes Tabby slept under her bed on the stacks of papers. Still no luck. She crept down the hall and slowly opened her parents' bedroom door. She stumbled upon her father, who was standing behind the door with a baseball bat ready to smash the "burglar" he had heard in the basement. "Josie! What the hell are you doing?" he yelled and Martha came out of the closet where she had been instructed to hide.

"I'm looking for Tabby. She's missing," Josie said innocently.

"Nonsense! Go back to bed, it's too early to be up roaming around all over the house," Herman said as he put the hand-carved bat back under his side of the bed.

Josie went back to her room and wondered how much trouble she might be in if she went outside to look for Tabby. Her father wasn't against spanking her with a belt. Josie thought belt spankings hurt less than when he used his hand. Her best friends, Danny and Adam, agreed. Their dads had a mean open palm spank. Josie tried to figure out the boundaries before her dad took such measures. Talking back to her mother had been the main reason for such spankings, whereas getting lost or forgetting the time and showing up after dark had mainly earned her only threats. When she would return unharmed, Herman usually took off his belt and held it in his hands, but never came near Josie. She wondered about her chances if she left the house. It would be disobeying a direct order, and also she might get lost searching for Tabby. Now she reckoned she better wait until it was light out.

"My room has too many corners in it," Josie said as she shined her new flashlight around. "I can't see the whole room from one point of view. There are way too many hiding places. I'd like a bedroom where I could see the whole room from my bed."

Josie crawled into bed with a Nancy Drew book and her flashlight and began reading. Soon after, distracted about her dream from the other night, she took out her notebook and started doodling. She was startled awake when her mom appeared in the doorway and said, "I can't seem to find Tabby either." Blinded by the sun shooting through the gap in her curtain, she found herself covered in books and wondered how she ever slept with Tabby missing.

"Let's go outside and look," Josie said as she bounced out of bed, tossing the books aside and stepping directly into her slippers.

"You'll need your boots, honey. And be quiet, your father is still sleeping. He was out late on a case."

Josie cocked her head with a confused look and wondered why she didn't hear the phone ringing, or have any dreams.

"Dad's not going to draw a gun on us if we go sneaking out, is he?" Josie said playfully, letting go of her concern over the missed called.

"No silly, I don't allow guns in this house and it's morning now, so he won't be thinking we are criminals."

They combed the neighborhood for Tabby. Josie continuously walked around their one square block and she searched the shrubbery, look up each tree. After losing her grandmother, Josie was skeptical if she would ever see her cat again. She believed if they found her, Tabby would be bald and dead like her grandmother. Josie tried to drag her mother up to the barn about a quarter mile up the road, which could be seen from their house, but her mother said she needed coffee before such an adventure. So Josie pleaded to go alone, which Martha reluctantly allowed.

Josie loved the field surrounding the barn in the spring. At that time of the year it was full of dandelions and wild flowers, but right then it was crunchy and tiny drying thistles were sticking to her pants. She picked them off as she meandered towards the barn.

With a high-pitched "kitty-kitty," Tabby reluctantly emerged from the haystack. Josie was dismayed to find her shacked up with a scruffy black cat. It took a moment for Tabby to come out of the haystack and greet Josie. Tabby was a fat, longhaired, lazy tabby that cried when she got stuck up in trees, and relied on her humans to save her. Josie could not imagine her surviving alone in the wild even for one night. Josie imagined that being a renegade house cat staying in a barn with a dingy farm cat would be parallel in the cat world to her staying in a hotel with room service. Josie assumed Tabby got the large brut looking male to hunt for her; she was not much of a hunter. Josie couldn't recall Tabby even killing a bug, maybe pawing at it, but never following through with bug murder.

Josie figured by finding Tabby, she had saved her from a vagrant lifestyle, hiding out in a wild unincorporated farmstead, dining on fresh kills, and living in sin, in an unkempt barn. As Josie picked her up, Tabby purred and was probably pretty pleased to be headed home to uninterrupted napping on Berber carpet and endless eating of canned salmon.

With Tabby curled in her arms and a big smile on her face, Josie turned to exit the barn. When her eyes adjusted to the sun pouring in from the barn doors, she saw a dead woman hanging from the rafters. She screamed and Tabby jumped from her arms, claws out, and scratched Josie's arms. Josie stood frozen with her arms bleeding through her flannel pajamas.

———

"You let her go where by herself?" Herman yelled at Josie's mother back at the house.

"I can see the barn from here. She just went out of my sight for the first time. She's gone there plenty of times before with Danny and Adam."

"Well, I'm going to go get her," Herman said and slammed the back door making Martha jump.

Herman found Tabby running towards the house as he crossed the field halfway to the barn. When he heard Josie yelling, "Dad!" he started to run.

Josie had not seen her dad in the field. She hadn't taken her eyes off the dead woman. She just knew that her dad needed to be there, so she started yelling. Herman came rushing in, out of breath and said, "Josie, are you okay? I saw Tabby running back home." He then noticed the blood on her clothes. "What happened?"

Staring at the body, Josie was still frozen. "I don't know," Josie mumbled while her dad squatted down looking at her arms with his back was to the body.

"Well, let's get you home and cleaned up." Herman touched her arm, but she didn't move or change the direction of her stare. Herman tugged at her.

"Don't we need to call the police?" Josie said not budging.

"Josie, what are you talking about?" Herman said.

Then, Josie pointed to the hanging woman.

Herman turned around and quickly turned back and pulled Josie to his legs and shielded her face, so she couldn't see the body anymore. "Okay Josie, here's what we're going to do. You're going to keep your eyes closed and hold my hand until we get out of the barn. I'll tell you when you can look. It's just like Grandma used to do. Okay?"

"Okay."

"Here we go." Herman guided Josie out of the barn and then told her she could open her eyes. Then he instructed her to run all the way home and have mom call the State Police. "Don't stop for Tabby, she'll find her way home."

Josie burst forward in a full sprint though her boots were clumsy to run in, and she went as fast as she could. Her mom had seen Tabby and was in the field retrieving her when Josie came running. Martha had picked up Tabby, noting she smelled like a barn and might need a bath. And lamented that this was not an easy task.

As Josie approached, loudly panting and out of breath, Tabby leapt from her mom's arms, scratching her too, and started running towards home.

Her mother yelped and asked, "What's wrong Josie? Why is Tabby so scared?" Her mom looked up from her own bleeding arm and glanced at Josie. "You're bleeding, too. What happened? Where's your father?"

"Mom, we need to call the police," Josie said while gulping for air.

"What? What's happened to your dad?" Her mom's eyes widened with concern.

"Nothing. There's a dead woman in the barn," Josie said without a hint of fear.

"Josie, stop telling stories," she said in a demanding a motherly tone. "Where is your father?"

"No, Mom. He's waiting with her body. We have to call his work."

"What?"

"Someone was murdered in the barn! I'm not telling stories!"

"Okay." Her mom looked stunned and glanced back at the barn.

"Let's go!" Josie yelled and started to run as her mom followed at a slower pace.

Josie dialed the State Police Post number on the wall over the phone, and held out the phone while waiting for her mom to enter the kitchen.

Before her mom reached the phone, Josie could hear the woman on the phone saying, "Can I help you? Are you alright?"

Martha grabbed the phone from Josie's extended arm, "This is Martha Banks. My husband is with the Bridgeport Regional Laboratory. He needs you to send his team and the police to the dead-end at Center Woods Drive, the barn at the end of the road. He found a body."

"I found the body!" Josie yelled out.

"Yes that's right, my little girl found the body. Herman is with it now. We're back home."

While Tabby circled her legs, Josie stood by the back-door staring out towards the barn, waiting for the police to arrive. There were sirens in the distance, but she wasn't sure where they were headed. Maybe there was a fire too, she thought. But then she saw police cars speeding up her street. Tossing her head the other direction, she looked across the field, and her dad popped out of the barn and waving the police over. Seconds later Martha instructed Josie to stay in the house and away from the windows, since her mom didn't want her seeing the woman in a body bag. Josie reluctantly complied and went to her room to draw out the crime scene.

Assuming her house would soon be filled with the State Police officers, Martha frantically cleaned the downstairs and then went upstairs to shower. She stopped by to check on Josie, giving her big hugs, which Josie didn't pause her drawing to receive. Martha suggested that Josie clean up her room. Martha believed making her clean would keep her distracted from thinking about the dead woman. Although Martha didn't quite understand the workings of Josie's mind. She didn't know that Josie had movie-like images playing all the time and simple tasks such as cleaning only sharpened these images. Josie didn't have a way to distract herself or quiet her mind. A pencil or brush was the best tool she had to erase bad memories.

Still focused on her house being overrun by officers soon, Martha showered and put on a simple blue dress, which she thought made her look taller than she was. Mindlessly she dabbed on a bit of blush, but then decided not to fuss and let her long black hair air-dry. Martha thought she would be less nervous if she didn't look like a stressed-out mom in a plain housedress, but didn't want to look like she cared too much. She went back into Josie's room, and she stood in the doorway and watched Josie drawing before she interrupted and asked to see the picture.

"It's not done yet, Mom. I can't show you," Josie said in a firm but slightly frantic voice.

Martha didn't want to push her. "Okay, honey. Let's take a break though. I'm…"

Josie interrupted, "In a minute. I almost have the barn done."

"I'm going to start some oatmeal cookies. If you want cookie dough you better be down before I put them in the oven."

Josie smiled and eagerly said, "I'll be fast."

"I knew the cookie monster in you would come out," Martha teased, tousling Josie's hair as she got up. She kissed Josie on the top of her head, hoping she had finally discovered a distraction for her daughter to forget — at least for a little while.

—

"So Josie found the body?" asked Bridgeport State Police Detective Joe White.

"I don't want Josie interviewed." Herman said sternly. "She's been through so much with her grandmother passing."

"Procedure calls for it, Herman."

"Well, let me talk to her first."

"Okay, I can break that protocol. But we need you off this case. Too close to home, for many reasons. Why don't you go talk with Josie and I'll be up with Sandy in a bit. Josie likes Sandy, right? I heard they were pals at the last work picnic."

"Josie is fond of Sandy — talked about her for days after that picnic." The detective nodded as Herman walked away.

After being instructed to leave again by another officer, Herman crossed the field in the direction of the house, looking a bit deflated. His wife paced by the door, spilling the coffee on her dress that she had poured for Herman when she saw him coming towards the house. Wide-eyed she met him at the backdoor with a half full cup of coffee. Her hand shook as she held out the cup that she hoped would give him some comfort. Blatantly dismissing the gesture he briskly walked towards the stairs, and all Martha could think to say was, "Now Josie may miss another week of school." Herman didn't respond, went straight to Josie's room and closed the door.

"Dad!" Josie jumped up. "What's happening over there? Did they get her down yet?"

"Josie, don't worry about that." He gently put his hands on her shoulders and directed her to sit back down on the bed. "We need to talk about what you saw when you arrived at the barn, so that you can tell the detective the story too." Josie didn't start there — she told her father that she didn't have a dream about a hanging woman. Last night, her dream was just about her dad and her walking together somewhere familiar. Nothing about crimes. "Josie, you don't need to tell *them* about your dreams. That's between us for now. Just tell them what you saw in the barn."

"So they don't know about my dreams?"

"They do, Jo but I don't want them coming to you to solve all of their cases. I need to protect you. That could put you in danger."

"But if I help catch the killers, then there is no danger."

"Well, Josie that's sort of true but... I'll explain that later. Now about the barn, what happened when you arrived?"

"I saw Tabby jump down from the top of the haystack with another cat. A big, black cat."

"Did you hear anybody else in the barn?"

"No." Josie had been focused on Tabby, and at that point she hadn't really even looked around the barn.

"Did the other cat look hurt in anyway?"

"No. Can't you find that cat? I'm sure he lives there. Why else would Tabby go there?"

"I'm sure they'll find him." Herman touched Josie's arm to calm her down and keep her focused. "Now, when did you see the woman?"

Josie went on to describe in slow motion each of her steps and turns, as though she was a dancer on stage. When actually she had just turned around normally, screamed, and then didn't move. What she didn't tell her dad was that she tried to memorize the woman's features, so she could draw her. Most of her drawings had been from dreams that replayed in her mind. She didn't really know how to keep this image accessible. So she pretended her mind was a camera and took a bunch of photos. Her drawing ended up looking like a crime scene drawing by a professional sketch artist. "It's not finished," Josie said as she pulled out her drawing and gave it to her dad. He studied it with concern and then rolled it up.

"Okay, Detective Joe White and Sandy are going to come up. Are you ready to tell them what you saw? Just what you saw today, okay?" Herman quickly unrolled and tucked the drawing into a bookcase.

"I'm ready." Josie fidgeted nervously and stared at the shelf where the drawing was now hidden between two books, its crisp edge poking up barely noticeably. With her grandmother's uncanny ability to always sense the truth, Josie found no use for lying and was horrible at it. But really she thought this wouldn't be lying, just not talking about other stuff, she told herself as she fiddled with a pencil. She also wondered what was in the drawing that her dad didn't like.

Martha straightened her dress before greeting Detective White and Sandy at the front door. She tried her best at small talk but could tell it was falling short as Detective White interrupted and asked where Josie was. Herman was halfway down the stairs when he heard Detective White. He yelled down, "She's up here. Come on up." Martha was hoping they would talk in the kitchen since she really hadn't cleaned well upstairs. Sandy and Detective White started up the stairs, Martha yelled up, "Do either of you want coffee?"

Sandy politely responded, "No, thank you. We are fine," as she rounded the corner of the hallway. Martha paced in the kitchen.

"Hi. Josie," Sandy said softly as she squatted down in front of Josie.

Josie smiled and shyly said, "Hi." Then asked, "How is your puppy?"

"She's big now. You'll have to come see her soon."

Josie turned to her dad, "Can we?"

Herman nodded.

"Josie, can we ask you a few questions about the barn?" Sandy asked.

Josie nodded.

Detective White abruptly jumped into the conversation, shifting seats to be closer to Josie, "Why did you go over to the barn this morning?"

Herman leaned in close, directly across from Josie as Detective White asked her a series of questions. Josie repeated what she had told her dad and didn't mention any dreams. Seemingly satisfied with what were normal ramblings from a little girl's experience, though Josie did make it sound more like a big adventure than something scary, Herman and the officers went downstairs. Herman had instructed Josie to stay in her room a bit longer. She tried to listen through the vent to her mom being interviewed, but they sat in the living room, which was not directly under Josie's room, so she sat with Tabby by the window overlooking the pines bordering her backyard.

"Why were you out there, Tabby?" Josie asked as she scratched under Tabby's chin. "You never go that far from home on your own, just that old lady's house a few doors down, because she gives you treats. Did you follow that woman there? I thought you were inside last night, when did you get out? I really wish you could talk — this purring is not translatable."

Later that night, when everyone was in bed, Josie took her new flashlight and snuck out the back door with Tabby on her heels. She wanted to see if she had missed anything in the barn for her drawing. As they crossed the field, the weeds that had scratched her in the morning, now damp, soaked through her pajama pants. She noticed that Tabby was tentatively following behind. Josie figured she had followed someone last night — it was not like Tabby to sprint off this far from home. Maybe it was the lure of the black cat.

The area was roped off but Josie easily slipped under the twine and ventured inside the barn. It smelled different than it had that morning. Where a musty scent had lingered, it now smelled clean. What did they clean? Josie wondered. She kicked up dirt as she slowly shuffled around the barn. She shined her flashlight towards the haystack, and wondered why her father had asked if she saw anything else. What had she missed? Had someone been in the barn with her? She poked around in the corners, which seemed to have been thoroughly searched by the cops. She lit up the area where the woman had been hanging. The yellow circle of light from the flashlight lit up the empty space like a spotlight at the circus illuminating the place where something had just disappeared. As the light flickered a bit Josie imagined the body swaying. Her stomach sank. Tabby frantically circled at her feet, rubbing her cheeks against Josie's leg — marking her with her scent, almost protectively. Josie looked down, but ignored her and wondered how did he get her up there? Maybe he brought a ladder and then took it back? There must have been a car then. Or a neighbor? Dad is always saying you never know who lives down the block, so you need to be careful everywhere. A car seemed more likely, but who would drive to this spot? A dead-end seemed like a place you'd get caught in a chase. Maybe he wanted me to find the body.

Josie stood still, shining the flashlight around the corners of the barn. She was startled this time when Tabby rubbed against her legs. When she looked down it wasn't Tabby but the black cat. When Josie slightly shifted her foot as she bent over to pet him, and he lashed out, hissed, and took off running. She tried to follow him with the flashlight to see where he went, but lost him in the hay piles. Josie wondered if someone had kicked him, because her boot seemed to have spooked him. She looked around, searching for where the black cat had hidden from the police. Josie felt a chill and thought she should have worn a coat and then Tabby ran out of the barn towards home. The black cat pounced from the haystack, Josie let out a scream and she took off running after Tabby. Josie's father was half way across the field picking up Tabby when Josie approached him out of breath.

"Josie!" He said sternly. "Get inside!"

"Dad, I just…"

"I don't want to hear it, you can't be outside at night by yourself. The world is not a safe place for little girls to just be wandering around in the dark with a flashlight."

"I'm sorry, Dad. I just wanted…"

"I don't care what you wanted. You can't be doing it. How am I going to protect you if you're out there," he pointed to the barn, "all by yourself and no one knows where you are?" Herman yelled.

Not sure if it was an actual question for her to answer, so she mumbled, "I don't know."

"That's right Josie, you don't know. I know. I know it's not safe. You think you're invincible just like my mother. And look what happened to her."

Josie started to cry and ran to the house and up to her room — she slammed her door before Tabby could

get in. Tabby sat in the hall and cried until her mom opened the door.

"Josie, what's happening? Why are you slamming doors at this hour?"

Unable to speak, Josie cried and shook her head. Martha twirled and tucked Josie's pin-straight hair until she fell asleep with Tabby and her flashlight tucked in close.

⌐

Since the late-night barn incident, Martha hadn't let Josie out of her sight. Though she fully intended to spoil her daughter and take her shopping and to museums, Martha was exhausted from all of the constant worry. When Martha could muster up the energy they did small art projects in the craft room in the basement. Josie finally begged to go outside. Martha watched nervously by the window as Josie roamed around the yard.

Michigan's autumns always have had a distinct smell, a combination of fallen maple, oak, and honey locust leaves. The spicy mixture floated up to Josie's nose, she breathed in a delight nearly as delicious as the scent of freshly baked cookies. This smell was compounded when she raked the leaves into a big pile, which was something Josie's grandparents would do with her each autumn. Martha had a photo of Josie, not even two, gleefully smiling as she was tossed into an enormous bed of leaves.

Josie's parents were too busy to neither rake nor have any interest in making a huge pile of leaves just for fun, so

Josie decided to do it herself. Josie was almost too old and too big to be tossed into her giant mound of mingled maples and honey locust leaves, but when Herman got home that day she pleaded for him to pick her up and toss her in. Herman was skeptical, and predicted it would be more like a thud against the ground rather than the memories Josie had of floating through leaves. Josie didn't care. So, a one, two, *and* three and Josie was up in the air and then floating down fast through the pile. And buried. That's when Herman yelled, "Don't move, Josie. I need to photograph this." So Josie stayed still in the middle of the pile with just her face poking through the gold, orange, and red leaves. Josie thought maybe she looked cute and that was why her dad ran for his camera. Quickly returning and as he fumbled to load the film, he mumbled on about how the head naturally floats to the top when someone is buried alive.

"Buried alive?" Josie said as she rustled in the leaves.

"Don't move, Josie! I need to get this shot first."

"People bury people alive?"

"Some do." Herman said with the camera in front of his face.

"Do people get out? Is it like climbing out of a pile of leaves?"

"Some do. And not really. Dirt is much heavier than leaves."

"Can I get out now? I think I feel spiders on me."

"Struggle a bit and then pause."

Josie did as she was told and then burst out scratching her legs, looking for spiders. There were none but Josie went inside and made her mom double check.

⌐

After seeing Josie having fun in the leaves, Herman instructed Martha let her play like a normal kid for a bit instead of being under house arrest. So a few days later, Josie was still off school and her mom allowed her go to the neighbor's house. Josie's best friends, Adam and Danny, were at school, though, Yvonne, who went to Catholic school, was off for the day.

Josie loved playing outside at Yvonne's. Yvonne had an oak tree that took up half of the front yard and seemed larger than her family's split-level 1960s brick home. This hardwood tree had low, wide branches and with a slight running leap you were up one story. Yvonne and Josie liked to climb up as far as they could, until fear halted their ascent. It wasn't the height that scared them, but the belief that Yvonne's father would punish them for their daredevil carelessness.

Yvonne's house and the massive tree were about two blocks from Josie's house. Just another half of a block away there was an open circular field of trees, mostly pines. But Yvonne's tree was the only one Josie was interested in climbing since her father took down her tree house. Josie fell out of it once while flapping her arms like wings too close to the edge. So her mother had forbidden her to go up and demanded that Herman remove the ladder nailed into the tree trunk. Josie was left with two honey locust trees in her front yard, which had no low branches. They both had long trunks with deeply grooved bark and their massive branches forked off into smaller and smaller branches, but there was no way up. The honey locusts were useless to Josie, and they made a mess every autumn. Soon after the first frost, flat banana shaped pods littered her front lawn until Herman commanded Josie to pick them up before they rotted and damaged his pampered crabgrass-free lawn.

Josie had no responsibilities regarding Yvonne's tree. Its massive size and shape resembled a fairy tale tree in a children's book, a fantasy world, one place Josie could escape all her dark thoughts. In the spring they caught fuzzy caterpillars crawling on the branches, watched ladybugs munching on the leaves, and in the fall they collected red leaves like they were pieces of gold. Mainly they hid up high for hours, convinced no one could see them.

Yvonne's tree was a white oak with oversized acorns that they used to chuck at the older neighbor boys. They had no romantic interest in boys yet. On this particular day off from school, bundled in winter clothes, in a bare tree, Josie sat on a branch wedged close to another so she had a back support. She ran her fingers along the jagged edges of one of the few remaining brown leaves as Yvonne talked about what she wanted to be when she grew up. Nonetheless Josie was pretty sure Yvonne was going to have babies and be a housewife like her own mother. Josie was also convinced that Yvonne's brother was going to be a mad scientist. He had the strangest collection of snakes, spiders, and mice, plus his room was full of dismantled electronics. He was older and wouldn't talk to them.

Josie wasn't thinking about growing up yet. She was still thinking about how to help solve her dad's case. "Did you hear about the woman in the barn?"

"I did," Yvonne responded, but she was still engrossed in peeling a dried leaf apart.

"Well, I think she was pretty, but her neck was broken and it…"

"I don't want to hear about it. Your stories always gross me out," she said without taking her eyes off the leaf in her hands.

Yvonne didn't have the stomach to talk about dead bodies. There were rumors that her dad was in the mob, so Josie figured that crimes were secret in their home, unlike the open discussion in own house.

# 6

After a month of strange incidents, Josie was beginning to think that her grandmother was haunting her. She worried about asking her mother if ghosts were real, because she didn't want to have to answer any questions about what she had seen or heard. But she mustered up the courage and tried to inquire casually about the subject. "Do you believe in ghosts?"

"Of course not, honey. Ghosts are just in your imagination and in stories." Then her mother went back to working on her Christmas cards that were late, which Josie only knew because her mother kept ranting that the barn incident got in the way of all of the holiday plans. It had been Martha's yearly ritual: long nights at the dining room table writing letters to everyone she knew, which were few. Josie wasn't sure why it took her so long. They also missed their yearly trip to Bronner's Christmas Wonderland. Herman normally grumbled the whole time the family strolled around the historical town of Frankenmuth. His lack of excitement for Christmas decorations and a feast of Josie's favorite fried chicken at Bavarian Inn put a halt to it this year, mainly since he didn't have to tell his mother he didn't want to go. It had been a holiday family tradition starting when his father fell in love with covered bridges back in the 40s.

Despite her mother's skepticism about ghosts, Josie was convinced that either she had inherited her grandmother's psychic powers or her grandmother was hovering close by. She liked it when her grandmother seemed to be helping with her spelling tests. That moment when Josie would struggle to remember the word and then pop, the answer would just come to her even though she hadn't studied. No one seemed to notice that she had been studying less and less since the nightmares started. She used to love to stay up reading and working on her homework, but lately she was too tired. The dreams took a lot out of her. As much as she didn't really want to go to sleep and confront them, she felt like something was tugging her, dragging her to bed. Her normal routine would be to fall asleep immediately and then wake up in a cold sweat. And then she would get up and draw what she had seen and immediately afterwards go back to sleep. This pattern repeated several times a night.

There were the nights when all she heard in her head was her grandmother singing her to sleep with a gentle lullaby. Josie had listened closely but couldn't make out the words, just the low hum of her grandmother's voice. It was comforting, until one night she heard her grandmother yell, "No! Not yet! No!"

Josie jumped out of bed, tripping over her books, and Tabby cowered in a corner. Josie ran past her hissing cat down the hall to her parents' room. "Grandmother is in trouble," Josie yelled.

Her dad sat straight up in bed. "What? Where?"

Josie's mom burst into tears and forced out the words, "Herman, Serena is dead." She said it sharply to bring him out of his dreamy state, but was too harsh for Josie, who began to cry. "Josie, your grandmother died a month ago, don't you remember?"

"I do," Josie said faintly.

"It must have just been a dream," Herman grumbled.

"Do you want to talk about it, honey?" Her mother asked after shooting Herman a look for his grumbling.

"No." Josie wasn't convinced they would understand since they didn't seem to believe in ghosts, and her dad didn't even really believe her grandmother had special powers. Josie slowly walked out of her parents' room as her mother called out, "Do you want me to tuck you in?" Josie mechanically shook her head no.

                    ⟵

In bed with her eyes wide open, Josie was scared to go back to sleep. That deep yelp her grandmother let out was scarier to her than dreams about her dad's murder cases. The thought of something bad happening to her grandmother terrified Josie. And since she felt like her grandmother was still with her all the time, this fuss about her being dead really didn't mean much to Josie. Josie felt like her grandmother was more present than before. Now she was a constant companion instead of a guest at weekly Sunday dinners.

Josie reluctantly went back to sleep, almost without a choice. Despite the fact that she had left all the lights on, left her record player playing, and had a coloring book out on her lap, she still fell asleep. "Josie, Josie, I have to go," her grandmother's soft voice said. "Sweet Josie, I can't visit any longer. Josie, can you hear me? You will be safe. No matter what happens, you will be safe. Just do what's right in your heart. I love you. Goodbye, sweet Josie."

"Wait!" Josie yelled as she opened her eyes. She heard the thump of quick footsteps from down the hall and her parents rushed into the room.

"What happened, Josie? Are you okay?" Martha asked shakily.

"She's gone! She left."

"I know, Josie. It's hard. Everything will be okay." Her mother's words or her grandmother's didn't convince Josie. She could sense that if her grandmother was really gone, something bad was going to happen. Maybe her father was right that his mother couldn't save his brother — it was too personal, like a mirror held too close. And now with her grandmother gone, Josie knew she had to be brave, so her powers wouldn't diminish, like her grandmothers did, as the violence grew closer to home.

⌐

Josie was in Mrs. Clemens' class for a second year in a row. All though she wasn't held back, Mrs. Clemens taught second and third grade together. Some of Josie's classmates complained at this point in the school year that they wanted a new teacher, and that they were bored with the same one as last year, but not Josie. She loved Mrs. Clemens, who was warm and gave big enveloping hugs like Josie's grandmother had. Josie's mom was bony and thin and not a big hugger, but Josie was. So much so that she hugged strangers when they looked like they needed one, which was another habit her mother was trying to break her of.

It was Josie's first day back to school, after her grandmother's death and the recent incident in the barn. Mrs. Clemens had been given a full report about everything that had happened, but Josie didn't know that and wanted to tell her everything at recess time.

"So my cat ran away." Josie said as she sat next to her teacher on a bench while the other kids in her class played on the monkey bars and swings.

"I heard." Josie didn't inquire how. She thought maybe Mrs. Clemens was like her grandmother and just knew things.

"Tabby found something."

"I heard."

"I wasn't scared. I'd seen dead bodies just a few days before in the funeral home. I knew the woman was dead as soon as I saw her hanging up there." Josie said almost with excitement, which seemed to concern her teacher.

"Well, seeing your grandmother in a casket is different than what you saw in the barn, isn't it?"

"Oh, I saw lots of dead bodies at the funeral home, in the basement," Josie said like it was still a secret.

"You did? Who took you to the basement?" Mrs. Clemens crinkled her brow and almost seemed angry that someone would take her there.

"No one. I wanted to talk to my grandmother, so I went down when my dad was buying the casket. He hates spending money and didn't know I was gone."

Mrs. Clemens eased up her rigid posture and felt relieved that Josie's dad didn't take her to the morgue. She had heard about the visits to the Lab. "Oh, I see. Was it scary down there?"

"No, just real cold. And the guy that worked there said that I upset the dead by talking to them like they were alive. I suppose that was a bit scary. But the dead people just looked like they were sleeping with lots of makeup on. My grandmother never wore that much makeup before. She looked like a doll."

"Well, you know your grandmother has passed away and can't talk anymore? Just like dolls can't talk," Mrs. Clemens said gently.

"Yeah, but she spoke in the hospital when she looked dead, so I thought maybe she would again. It was worth a try, but no luck. But she did hear me though. She has been coming to me in my dreams like I asked. The dreams with crime scenes are starting to look more like movies with sound and everything. And they're starting to scare me less, especially if I get up right afterwards and draw about them. It helps not to carry them in my mind all the time, on paper is good, so I can figure out how to help solve the crime."

Mrs. Clemens stopped watching the children on the playground and focused all of her attention on Josie. "What crime, Josie?"

"I think this most recent dream may be about the case my dad is working on now. It has all the same stuff. I now can see who it was that shot the gun."

"So are there guns in all your dreams?" The pitched changed in Mrs. Clemens' voice. She was freaking out that this sweet girl had all this second-hand violence in her world.

"No no. The one before there was just something going on in the field. I think it's the same field where they found the dead girl though. I saw the bunny. But I couldn't get close enough to see what was across the field. But like I said, they're becoming more like movies, so maybe I can see the whole thing soon."

"You know Josie... I'm..." Mrs. Clemens didn't know how much she should press about the dreams. Just then the bell rang, and Josie jumped up and ran inside.

It was art time, and Josie hurried to get the best paint-brushes. With all of her doodling in the middle of the night and during class, Josie was starting to construct the outside of the shed where the woman was shot. She thought maybe she could paint the whole crime scene, the dragging of the body through the leaves and everything. She heard her fa-ther say on the radio that they didn't know where Lorraine was killed and that her body had just been dumped in the woods. In the tiny moments that the gun went off and lit up the whole room, Josie could see the shooter's face. She want-ed to paint that clearly today too if there was time.

At the big table by the windows, Josie sat alone. Her best friends, Adam and Danny, were both out sick that day. Adam was a cute, freckle-faced, curly haired, short boy who could dribble a soccer ball circles around Josie. When Josie was six years old and played on an opposing boys' team, she chased his fancy footwork up and down the field and rarely caught him.

Danny was an olive-skinned, lanky boy who could out-run anyone in elementary school. Each timed race in gym class, Josie tried with all her might to beat his record, but she never came close. When instructed to line up and pair up back in kindergarten, it was either Adam or Danny hold-ing her hand. The three of them were together every chance they could get; on their dead-end street, on the dirt hills at Demeter, rainy afternoons in Josie's basement playing ping-pong, and riding bikes on the trails in the woods just beyond the barn.

Josie could be very selective about whom she connected with at school. Once she told Mrs. Clemens that she really liked all the kids in the class and said, "I think they like me, but they wear me out." Some days nearly mute, Josie made herself invisible at school unless someone asked her about books or crime. On occasion she could be found with a circle of boys around her when she told stories about murder.

———

"My dad found a man in the do-it-yourself car wash on Hemlock Street." The boys drew closer. "Shot in back. He was face down with the water hose in his hand but no car."

One of the boys chimed in, "Someone must've took his car."

"My dad says that doesn't prove that there was a car there at the time. They need a witness."

Another boy asked, "Did the man own a car?"

"They don't know who he is. So maybe he was homeless and washing himself."

Another boy said, "No that's crazy. There had to be a car and the killer took it."

"Maybe. But my dad said we're no longer allowed to go to those kinds of car washes." Most of the boys thought Josie made up the stories, but a few of them from school had seen that he drove an official State Police car.

Another time, Josie was trying to tell a story on about her fingernails. Most of the boys didn't care about her fingernails, but the girls showed a bit of interest. "My dad made me bite off my nails last night." She paused to see who might want to hear the whole story. One girl raised a single eyebrow. "Then he made me rip off the other set on this hand." Jose showed off her left hand.

"Why on earth would your dad make you do that?" said one of the girls.

"He needed them for a test at work. Some crime scene had a whole bunch of fingernails on the backseat of a car. Turns out the murdered girl's fingernails were snapped off."

"Gross, Josie I don't want to hear your murder stories." The girls turned all at once as a group and left.

Josie yelled after them, "My dad didn't make me do that." Josie couldn't understand their queasy stomachs about crime. But as her mom told her, when she was really little she also used to play with worms and bugs, which frightened away her older cousins. Undiscouraged, Josie preferred playing with boys — they seemed to share her love of "gross" things.

Josie started her painting with a rectangle and a slit for a door. Next she drew the outline of the man holding the gun pointed at Lorraine. It was the best view of the room — the other shots were closer to the body and only really lit up Lorraine's face. Josie's dad knew what Lorraine's face looked like, so she just kept that drawing simple with only a few lines for the nose and eyes. It was a bare room, almost like a shed with brick walls. Josie was staring at her painting and trying to figure out what color the cement was when Mrs. Clemens approached to check up on her painting.

"How is your painting coming along, Josie?" The assignment had been to pick an object in the room and paint it a different color than it actually was. Before Josie could answer, Mrs. Clemens audibly gasped but then calmly asked, "Do you see those objects in this room?"

"Oh no, Mrs. Clemens. These are for research, for my dad's crime scene. They don't know where she was killed..." Mrs. Clemens cut her off.

"Okay, Josie. Well, can I have your painting and give it to your dad?" She didn't want the other kids to see it and tell their parents.

"Sure, but make sure he gets it today. It's important that they find out where she was killed."

"Of course, Josie. I will." Mrs. Clemens tucked the painting in her desk. Josie worried that it wasn't dry yet but let it go when Mrs. Clemens announced it was cleanup time, which meant snack time was next. Each day Josie hoped some parent would be wise and make finger Jell-O, but healthy snacks were becoming the trend. It seemed to Josie that oats were always involved. Recently even for Josie's ninth birthday her mom made homemade granola bars, which only had a little bit of chocolate in them. But Josie was convinced it was those carob chips her mother was always trying to fool her with.

After school, Josie rushed home. She never had a chance to paint the gunman's face in class, and she wanted to draw it out at least before her mom and dad arrived home. She ended up finishing the whole painting before she heard her mom come home and start clamoring in the kitchen.

Martha was always hurrying, her tiny feet hitting the floor heavily in her big, white nursing shoes. For someone so small, only centimeters taller than five feet, she made a lot of noise. It was as if she spoke more loudly to make up for Herman's almost inaudible tone. Also in contrast Martha's clothes were loud. Before she worked so much she sewed. She sewed the curtains, her own clothes, and Josie's, but Herman insisted on buying all his clothes at Sears. She sewed doll clothes for Josie, and sewed napkins, tablecloths, and pillowcases. Most things she made with whichever fabric was on sale. Herman didn't like to spend money, so even though she was saving money by making things he still grumbled at the amount of the bill. Remainder fabrics were always a bit wild. With it being the '70s the patterns nearly jumped off the cloth. This didn't fit Josie's quiet nature. She often tucked the really loud dresses into the back of her closet. There was a time when Martha made nearly everything out of corduroy. Josie had to tell her it was too hot for corduroy sundresses. Martha protested that it was all she could afford to buy right now and somehow blamed Josie for growing so fast.

After slipping the painting in a secret place under her bed (a flat space between the support boards and the bed frame) Josie went downstairs to ask when dad was coming home. But she knew the answer when she saw the box of fried chicken. Her dad hated chicken, so it was just the two of them for dinner.

Josie frowned. "Is Dad out on a new case?"

"Yes, honey. We'll have to do something fun on girls' night."

Josie's mind went wild wondering what her mom meant by fun. Dance parties were common when her grandmother was still alive. Her grandmother could do the twist with such flare with her big hips and fancy skirts. Josie always tried to twist with so much speed she looked like a toy top spinning. Then she thought maybe they would go out somewhere; her dad rarely liked to leave the house in the evenings unless it was for work. She and her mom would sometimes go to the Riverwalk in the summer, but it was a chilly December evening. Just as Josie was about to ask, her mom said, "I bought some hook rugs. I thought we could make those tonight." Josie excitedly grabbed the one with the butterfly and pulled open the box. She barely touched her chicken as she sat and latched yarn to match the colored pattern.

Her mom tried several times to get Josie to talk about how she was feeling about her grandmother and being back at school. But Josie was concentrating on the rug and felt determined to get one wing done before she had to go to bed. She wanted to take it in for show and tell next week, since Mrs. Clemens said she needed to bring in things the girls would like too. The last thing she had brought in was the footprint molds her father and her made. Before that it was a dead bird she had found on the way to school.

———

The next day, Adam had miraculously recovered from the flu, and they walked together as usual to school. "One of my drawings is missing from my room," Josie told him.

"So?"

"Well, it was one I was working on that showed what the killer looked like."

"What?" Adam stopped walking.

"Well, my dad asked me what he looked like a few days ago, and I couldn't remember, but now I did." Josie kept up her brisk pace to keep warm.

Adam ran to catch up. "How? How did you remember?"

"I don't know how. It just came to me when I was walking to school yesterday."

"Are any more killers coming to mind while we walk now?" Adam said as he pretended to slowly back away from Josie.

Josie swatted at him, "No, I think it's because we're talking."

"Do you want me to be quiet?" Adam covered his mouth with his hands.

"No, silly! I want you to help me figure out who took my painting."

"Well, maybe your dad took it to work already."

"No, he didn't come home last night. He was on a case. Someone took it in the middle of the night and it was right under where I was sleeping. You would've thought I'd wake up. But maybe they took it before I went to bed?" Josie said like the last sentence had just occurred to her.

"So you think someone has been in your room?"

"I do. I think maybe the killer knows that I know what he looks like."

"Josie, who knows that you draw your crazy dreams?"

"Well, everyone at school. The whole police force. My mom, and I'm sure my aunts and uncles. My grandmother."

"Your grandmother's dead. Are you still talking to her like those imaginary friends you had when you were little?"

"She is nothing like imaginary friends, and I was talking about my other grandmother. The religious one, the churchy one, who thinks I need to be baptized so my dreams will go away. Her theory is a mild version of an exorcism. A little water on my head and I will be dreaming about ponies again."

"Oh, right."

"Then there's that older girl, Missy, up the street that my dad said I shouldn't talk to anymore because her dad has stacks of *Playboys* in the basement."

"Have any of those people been over? Who would break into your house for your drawing? I wouldn't. I was sick anyways."

"Adam, I don't think you did it. But I need your help to keep my drawings safe."

"Oh I've got it," Adam's eyes widened. Josie smiled excitedly at Adam's idea even before he said it. "We'll take big shoe boxes and burying them in the ground in each of our backyards. Danny's too."

"Perfect!"

It started to sleet and they picked up their pace to nearly a run, racing the rest of the way to school. Out of breath, Josie claimed she won and Adam said, "I didn't know we were racing." Josie spent most of the day at school focused on getting back home to look under her bed again for the painting, thinking maybe she overlooked it. Mrs. Clemens called on her several times, but she was distracted and didn't have the answers. Josie ran out of school when the bell rang at the end of the day, not even waiting for Adam. Mrs. Clemens took note of Josie's odd behavior and called her mom, asking her to stop by on her way home from work.

## Sparrow Street

When Josie got home, she noticed that other things had been disturbed under her bed. She was even more concerned that someone had been in the house. So she decided she needed to tell her mom, but really she wanted to call the police to have her room fingerprinted.

"Mom, someone stole something from my room," Josie said as she approached Martha in the kitchen, seconds after she arrived home. Josie didn't know if her dad had told her mom about the paintings so she tried to not tell the whole story.

"What did they take?" her mom asked while putting groceries away.

"A painting."

"You sure you didn't just misplace it? It can get pretty messy under your bed."

"How did you know it was missing from under my bed? Did you take it?" Josie turned all red in the face.

"No, Josie. I didn't take anything from under your bed. But I did see your drawing from Mrs. Clemens' class today. Is that the sort of painting that's missing?"

"No, the portrait I painted of the killer's face. It…"

"Josie, what killer?" Her mom stopped putting things away and looked at Josie.

"The one that shot that woman three times. The call Dad got the other night."

"So the killer from your dream?" Martha said while squatting down to speak eye to eye with Josie.

"Yes, but no. Dad told me to try to remember what he looked like. I don't ever remember seeing him in my dream, but I finally could on the way to school yesterday."

"Did you actually see the man on the way to school?" Josie's mom was a bit alarmed.

"No, just in my head." Josie was getting frustrated.

"So you made him up?" Josie's mom let out a deep breath and was relieved that Josie wasn't being followed. Thinking it might just be imaginary friends again.

"No! Mom. I have all the crimes inside of me. I can see everything."

"Josie, you need to stop all this silliness." Josie's mother's voice was getting louder and demanding.

"It's all inside of me. I just have to be still to see who the killer is."

They both turned when they heard keys jangling in the lock. The kitchen door opened and Herman grimaced at Martha's pained expression when he walked in the room. Herman looked exhausted, and appeared frustrated to find such a loud conversation, "What is she talking about, now?" Speaking directly to Marta and looking over Josie's head.

"She's saying that she just has to close her eyes and she can see who the killer is." Martha looked at Herman nearly in a panic attack mixed with rage towards him and fear for Josie's life.

"I don't even have to close my eyes anymore. Or dream. I just need to be still in my head and be here." Josie pointed to the ground like it marked a special spot.

Martha threw her arms up, and started pacing at the other end of the kitchen as Herman squatted down to talk to Josie.

"What do you mean by be here?" Herman asked meeting Josie's eyes directly.

"I'm able to see them when I kind of leave my body like a ghost costume with nothing under the sheet, and then I can clearly see other things that are out there." Josie pointed out the kitchen window. "Things that have happened. But I can't really see the future like Grandma could. As soon as I remember my name or something startles me out of it, it all goes away really fast."

"Is this something your grandmother taught you how to do?"

"No, I don't think so. I don't know how I do it. Like I just said to mom, I get really still and don't think about anything and then it starts like a movie."

Herman pulled her close to whisper. "Josie, I don't think you should be saying these things. It's hard for me to explain to you, but people will think you're lying. I know you're not, but not everyone can see their dreams when they're awake. For most people they fade as soon as they wake up. So just do the drawings in secret. No more showing anyone or talking about them. Just here at home. Okay?" Josie nodded her head yes. "Now let's have some dinner," Herman said and looked up searching for his wife, who was on the opposite end of the kitchen with her arms folded. Herman caught her eye and gave her a timid smile. Martha flung open the fridge without a return glance.

---

The Banks tried to have a normal family dinner and watch TV, but there was a noticeable tension in the room. Herman flipped the pages of his book loudly while he read during the commercials. Josie sat very quietly, while her mom couldn't help but think about what might be playing like a movie in her little girl's mind. Martha look relieved when Josie fell sound asleep on the floor in front of the TV. "Herman, take her upstairs before she has nightmares about this *Quincy* show."

———

"I think we need to send her to see someone," Josie's mom whispered to Herman as they settled in bed.

"I don't trust a psychiatrist with her."

"She's suffering. We need to do something to help."

"You can't protect her from all suffering. She'll have to face challenges in her life. We cannot protect her from everything." Herman said the last line with a bit of anger in his voice.

"But she doesn't have to see these crimes. She doesn't have to have this violence in her life at such an early age."

"I don't think it's our choice. I didn't give her the gift of dreams. Maybe my mother's genes did, but I don't have any psychic powers. And I didn't commit these crimes. This is the world, reaching her from the inside."

"I've been asking around at the hospital. There are a few good female psychiatrists that the doctors trust."

"You've been discussing her dreams with doctors at work?"

"No, not exactly. I'm concerned. This isn't like her invisible friends that just went away."

"I know and that's why we need to protect her. She has a gift. People will think she's a freak and want to use her for her gifts. I don't want the world knowing about this. I just need to figure out how to get her off track. Like my mother, she couldn't see everything. She didn't know my brother was going to crash. I've been thinking it had something to do with the violence being personal or too closely connected to her, and then she couldn't see who did it."

"But how do we get her to stop obsessing about this current case?"

"The Lab will solve it. Her obsession with the rabbit has gone away."

"I think that's only because this case scares her more."

"Maybe, but I don't think she's all that scared — she's brave."

"She is eight and seeing dead people. She's not you."

"My mother was never scared of her powers."

"You didn't know her when she was eight," Martha said firmly.

Herman said nothing else after that. There was only grumbling and a battle for blankets.

## The Lab

While the Banks' house was all tucked in for the night with no more mention of the missing drawing of the killer, one of the Bridgeport State Police detectives, Paul Williams, was up pondering the Owosso three-shots case. At almost seven feet tall and with large feet, he noisily paced around an eerily quiet Headquarters. He had headed over to the Lab to see if anyone was around. He saw someone inside the locked door of the chemistry lab where illicit drugs were identified. He stood out by the chemical exhaust hoods on the wall to the left of the door, waiting to be noticed. The room looked like something out of a science fiction film with neatly designed Herman Miller laboratory benches that stretch across the room. Each bench has reagent shelves in the middle and appropriate electrical and natural gas connections to use for Bunsen burners. At the opposite end of the room, from the door, is a smaller room containing instruments used for chemical analyses: infrared spectrometer, gas chromatographs, and mass spectrometer. The chemist never looked up from his instrument, so Williams gave up and went back to the Post. He decided the revolver found in the river was their best lead. He thought someone local must have been the second gun owner.

The following week Detective Williams dug deeper into the local Owosso gun records to trace the serial number. He went to every store that sold guns including Super City, which was essentially a discount store. It had a whole wall and cases of guns that were the target of many smash and grabs. Detective Williams, along with several local officers, went through all their paperwork. When they reached the second store, a sporting goods store, they figured out the owner of the gun. They confirmed his current address with the county and located Mr. James Dumont. Feeling pressed for the time, they skipped dealing with a small town judge and getting a warrant, and just confronted him at his home. Due to a solid alibi, confirmed with a few phone calls, they cleared him as a suspect in the crime.

The gun owner told police that he had *lost* the .22-caliber revolver many years earlier. But coincidentally he was able to provide them with the name of a man who was a "friend" of his former wife, whom he thought might possibly be linked to the crime and the gun. Several local officers berated him for not coming forward with this information before. They threatened him with obstruction of justice charges. The detective however calmed them down, saying the charges wouldn't stick.

Detective Williams called this a lucky break, but Herman thought maybe Mr. Dumont was trying to throw them off his trail. However, the information led investigators to a suspect that had been convicted and jailed for the 1961 rape and robbery of a blind University of Michigan student.

After quickly obtaining sperm samples from the old rape case, within a few days Herman had a match between the blood types and authorities located and arrested James Jansons on charges of premeditated felony murder. It appeared Jansons escalated to murder out of the fear of being identified. She was clearly blindfolded at one point, indicated by the bruising from a tight cloth and the shot in the back suggests she escaped. He may have never killed her since his history was for rape. It was his predisposition to sexual violence and his sperm that got him caught. Herman liked to think that his proper preservation of the specimen at the scene under the pine trees allowed this case to be solved. And since Herman was the investigator that collected and preserved the evidence, he was assigned to testify for the prosecution in the case. Josie pleaded to go to court and watch her father's testimony. Herman firmly told her that she couldn't be seen by any of the criminals, because it would be too risky. Since the case had also drawn local and national media attention, Josie heard there was a possible link to other rapes and murders and she wanted to help. While waiting for her father to return from court, Josie sat close in front of the TV, fixated on the local 5 o'clock news. Then there he was, Josie saw the killer and let out a high-pitched screamed. Her mother came running.

"That's him!" Josie pointed at the screen to the man in handcuffs walking past the press.

"Who Josie?"

"The man that grabbed me in my dream. The one in my stolen painting. The man that killed that woman curled up like a cat."

"Is that the case where your dad is testifying at?"

"Yes!"

Josie and Martha stared at the TV as a newscaster said, "James Jansons was found guilty and sentenced to life in prison without the possibility of parole."

Martha turned to Josie, "We don't have to think about him ever again. Okay, Josie. It's over. It's all over." Martha turned off the TV and held Josie and worried that maybe this wasn't over — which would confirm Martha's biggest fear.

# 7

At 3:30 a.m. Josie crawled out of bed with her pajamas all twisted and went into her parents' room to wake up her dad. "Dad, Dad, there is going to be a case tonight," she whispered. Herman was telling her to go back to sleep when the phone rang. Herman grabbed his robe and went downstairs to answer it. Josie crawled into bed next to her mom, who sleepily encouraged her to get under the covers by fluffing her dad's pillow.

Herman came back up and turned on the bedroom overhead light. Martha moaned at the light. "Josie, do you want to tell me about your dream before I go?" Herman asked in a formal business tone.

"Let her sleep, Herman," Martha whined.

"I'm awake." Josie sat up. "He stabbed her with a fork."

"What?" Herman and Martha said at the same time.

"Not an ordinary fork but one of those like grandpa used when carving the turkey." Josie gestured with her hands to show the size.

"Okay, Herman. I don't want to hear about this, let alone have Josie go over it again and again," Martha said fearfully.

"You're overreacting, Martha. Josie wants to help."

"I do, Mom. I'm not scared. I want to catch this guy."

"Josie, you're not catching anyone — that is the job of the police. Under no circumstances do you get involved with the case. Understood?"

Josie nodded. She figured if she didn't say yes out loud it was kind of like taking the fifth, which she had learned about while watching *Quincy* with her dad. She heard you couldn't be punished for anything later. Yet she had an odd feeling about this murder, a feeling she would be closely involved. The girl that was killed had been her babysitter. She didn't get a chance to tell her dad because her parents were arguing and then he had to leave.

Operations reported to Herman that when Mary arrived at her north side Saginaw home at three a.m., she found her teenage babysitter, dead on the living room floor. Herman arrived on the scene by four a.m. There was a small gathering of neighbors, news media, firemen, police officers, detectives, and brass waiting for the Lab to arrive. When Herman saw the teenage girl, brutally raped and stabbed to death, he gasped. It was Karen the babysitter he had hired a few months back. After seeing Herman's reaction a cop on the scene said, "It's just horrible, isn't it?" Herman played along that he too was upset about the fork wounds in her chest when really this one hit home personally.

The crime scene was littered with Karen's torn blue panties, her nearly shredded plaid skirt, and one large fork.

All Karen was left in was a once white sweater and white socks; her torn brassiere was inside her bloody sweater and a knife protruded from her throat.

As Sergeant Greg Adams, the latent print specialists, dusted for fingerprints, Herman surveyed the scene and began collecting trace evidence. No fingerprints were developed on the bloody knife and fork used as murder weapons. Frustrated at how the evidence was looking, Herman took a break, and called home from the phone hanging in the kitchen.

"Hi Martha. Can I talk to Josie?" Herman said like he was making a business call.

"What is this about? Is everything all right?" Martha's voice shook a bit. Herman had never called from a scene before even when his mother was sick.

"Yes. Everything is fine." Herman rolled his eyes and was annoyed he'd have to explain the reason for his call. "The evidence is looking slim, and I think Josie may be able to help on this one." For Herman to be this anxious this early in a case was unusual. He didn't even know if there was semen yet.

"I'm not sure about this, Herman. She seems upset today."

"Put her on, Martha." Martha put the phone down and yelled for Josie.

"Hi, Dad. It was Karen that was killed, wasn't it?" Josie had been stewing over this. Her grandmother said that the violence would never touch her. This felt too close, even closer than the woman in the barn. She felt scared like something was creeping in to hurt her, but she still wanted to help her dad.

"Yes, Josie. Do you know who did it?"

"Yes, I can draw him. But I think the little girl, who Karen was babysitting, saw him too."

"She's too scared to talk and that may take a few weeks. Can you draw him for me, and I'll pick it up on the way to the autopsy?"

"Okay, I'll start now." Josie put down the phone but didn't hang it up. She darted up to her room. Martha watched, standing nearly frozen, overwhelmed with anger towards Herman and not knowing how to help Josie.

"Thanks, Josie. I'll see in you an hour or so." Herman went to hang up the phone and saw the detective give him a look.

"Herman, you know the protocol. No using the phone at the scene," said the detective. Detective Roger Stevens seemed to be increasingly nitpicky with whatever Herman did. Herman wasn't sure when he had gotten on his bad side. It could have been a recent robbery case when Stevens interviewed a guy who failed a polygraph test, but Herman's fingerprint evidence didn't match the story the suspect told. He thought maybe because his evidence collection on the recent murder cases had been trumping any of Roger's detective work, there might be some jealousy. Herman had witnessed him mistrust other Lab employees that were not enlisted State Police officers. He seemed to only trust the Specialist Sergeants, who were specially trained in the forensic sciences. They mostly worked on pattern matching evidence such as polygraph, fingerprints, documents, and firearms identification. Since Herman was a civilian and mainly worked on trace evidence, Stevens was skeptical of his methods.

"It's about the case, sir." Herman tried to sound humble.

"Sounded like you were talking to your wife and kid."

"Well you've heard about Josie's dreams, right?" Detective Stevens nodded.

"They're getting more vivid, sir. I asked her to try to do a sketch of this killer. The…"

Roger cut Herman off. "This is all just crazy. How old is your kid again? She's having psychic dreams? And even if she is, she can't possibly draw that well, can she?"

"My mother put her in art classes when she was three. I thought she was training her to be a famous artist. I didn't know she would be doing portraits of killers." Herman wondered if his mother knew that she would need these skills exactly for this. He wondered why she didn't tell him all of this?

"This is not kid stuff. I don't want her involved in all of this. You're not feeding her details are you?"

"No. I don't think I can keep her out of this one. She woke me up before I received the call this morning to tell me someone was murdered. She also knew the victim. She babysat for us once, maybe twice," Herman said as he looked over his shoulder towards Karen's body.

"What the fuck? Okay, we need to keep her safe, put someone on your door. I've seen how obsessed people get with all this supernatural stuff. All the crazies come out. I'll talk to Lieutenant Gray."

"I can protect her, sir."

"You're not there right now, are you?"

"Point taken. Let me talk to my wife first. She won't like any of this." Roger nodded and turned away. Herman was pretty sure Roger would go straight to the Lieutenant and not wait for him to talk to Martha.

Herman continued to comb the scene for any bit of evidence. He found one foreign-looking head hair, which he recovered from the victim's left sock. Herman was fascinated with human hair. He wrote his final graduation essay on the subject. Several times he had cut and plucked Josie's hair for samples. Josie was thrilled to have slides made of her hair, which were then used in a classroom demonstration. She once took a slide to show-and-tell, but the other kids weren't impressed, even when Josie pleaded, "My dad can catch killers with these slides."

———

"Hey Herman, you done here? Let's go get that painting from Josie." Roger barked from across the room. So much for keeping things quiet, Herman thought.

Herman nodded towards Roger and followed behind to the detective's car and tossed the wagon keys to Greg. Herman worried about Martha's reaction to the detective coming to the house. He thought maybe he could get Roger to stay in the car. But really he wasn't sure he could get Roger to do anything that he wanted.

———

As they pulled into his driveway, Herman found it strange that Roger knew where he lived. Maybe he looked up the address while he was waiting for Herman to be done at the scene, Herman thought. "I'll just run in," Herman said as he opened the door before the car completely stopped.

When Herman got back in the car. Roger reached out for the painting, "Okay, let me see that."

Herman unrolled the painting. Josie had drawn the whole scene, including a photographic quality of the man's face standing over the body.

"Oh shit, maybe your kid really can see killers in her dreams. Fuck." Roger seemed a bit freaked out.

Herman wondered was it because he thought Josie was crazy or did he feel dumb that he didn't believe Herman? "Those are my thoughts too," Herman said feeling the need to break up the silence as Roger continued to stare at the painting.

"Let's take her to headquarters with us. I think we may need to interview her."

"Martha won't be pleased. You may need to come in and convince her," Herman reluctantly suggested.

"I can do that. I was a salesman before I joined the force. She'll agree," Roger said with confidence.

Martha didn't put up that big of a fight, since Josie was pleading with excitement to go as if she was visiting the zoo or circus. "I'll be safe there, Mom. And they need my help." Josie begged.

"Now Josie these men can solve the cases just fine on their own. I know you want to help but this is grownup stuff," Martha said almost to convince Herman and Roger that they didn't really need Josie for this one.

Josie looked at her dad. He nodded yes letting her know she could tell her mom.

"Karen was murdered and I…"

"Our babysitter?" Martha said in a panicked voice.

Detective Stevens jumped in, "Martha, why don't you come with us too. We need to discuss providing police protection for Josie."

Martha silently gathered her coat, grabbed Josie's, and joined them in the car.

Herman left Martha and Josie at Headquarters and went to photograph the autopsy. His film recorded bruises on the sides of the victim's face, and more knife and fork puncture wounds in her chest than were visible at the scene. This guy was in a rage — this anger could not have been for this girl, Herman thought. His mind flashed to Josie and he cringed that someone could do this to a young girl. He wondered if had put Josie in danger by having her do that sketch. Now with Roger handling the case, Josie is more involved than

I want. I hope it's only this case and not like my mother's freak-show childhood, Herman reflected. And just then as he had feared, Herman received a rare call in the middle of the autopsy. His secretary told him that the press had gotten wind that a young girl made an accurate sketch of the killer. Herman gasped, "They leaked that it was Josie didn't they."

"I'm sorry, Herman. They did."

"Damn it! This is going to turn into a circus show. I never should have let her go with Roger." Herman slammed his fist on the pathologist's desk. "Where is Josie now?"

"Roger took her and Martha home just a few minutes ago."

"Is he alone with them?"

"They just sent four officers to your house. She should be safe."

Reporters were outside Herman's house within minutes after someone from the State Police allegedly confirmed that it was Josie. Josie was scared and her mother was furious. Martha muttered angrily, circled inside the house, and called the Lab multiple times trying to get a hold of Herman. Two cop cars showed up. Four officers began searching the inside and outside of the house, pushing back the press off the property. Two cops stayed, one in front and one in back of the house. Martha made them coffee and asked them if they would radio Herman. They firmly said he was unreachable. Martha was skeptical that they were being truthful.

Herman came home later in the evening with two large pizzas. He knew the officers were there and would be hungry, even though he hadn't spoken to his wife.

"Why didn't you call me?" Martha started to yell then caught a glimpse of officer Daniel Johnson out of the corner of her eye and scaled back her tone.

"I didn't want to talk on a work line — where it may be recorded. Everything is recorded in that place. And I knew Johnson was here," Herman whispered.

"What are we going to do? Now everyone knows about her dreams. She can't even go to school," Martha said agitatedly, but managed to keep her voice down.

"She needs to go to school. She has to live a normal life," Herman said insistently.

"She's not normal," Martha argumentatively huffed. "Why does she need to do what normal children do all of a sudden?"

"Now don't let Josie hear you talking about her that way. She is perfectly comfortable with being different. And she likes school. It'll be good for her to keep going."

"I guess. If you think it is safe."

"We'll have officers at school. Josie will think that's cool. Now we should get some sleep." Herman nudged Martha towards the stairwell. "It's been a long day," Herman said as Martha shuffled up the stairs.

The next day Herman and Martha tried to make it a normal morning for Josie, but she was more interested in talking about the case with the cops, who she invited to the breakfast table. They resisted talking about the case, and instead strategized how to get Josie to school safely.

⌐⎯⎯

Officer Johnson was walking Josie home from school a few days later, and Josie skipped ahead and yelled back with excitement, "Look I got a package!"

Johnson pauses, "It's not your birthday, is it?"

"No, that was last month. January 3rd. You got me a present. The fancy markers."

"Right, right." Johnson paused thinking his wife must have sent them. "Then...Josie! Don't touch that!"

"But it has my name on it." Josie pleaded as she knelt down to look to see whom it was from.

"I know, but I need you to go inside, in the basement, take Tabby with you." Josie didn't argue. She could tell Johnson was serious. Johnson slowly opened the front door avoiding contact with the package. Once inside he hurried Josie along downstairs, she pretended to head down, but went back to the top step after he closed the door. Johnson called the department and told them there was a suspicious package on the front stoop of the Banks' home and he needed the bomb squad. Josie listened by the door. "A bomb," she whispered to Tabby. "We better stay here Tabby. They may bring the dogs."

Sirens blazing and Herman following in his state car, the parade of police cars rounded the corner of Sparrow Street at top speeds. The bomb squad cleared the press from across the street, putting up a roadblock. The dogs sniffed the box but didn't react as if there were explosives. One of the agents in protective army gear slowly carried the box to the middle of the street. Placed it down and slowly began to open the packaging. There was a box within a box. He called the dogs back to take another look. Still no response. As the agent carefully opened the second box he saw a wind up Jack-in-the-box toy. He tried to pry the top and one of the officers yelled, "You have to wind the damn thing. My kid is always trying to lift the top off but only winding works." The agent wound and wound and jumped when it popped. So did several other officers standing across the street. The toy was holding a note, which swayed with the springing motion, eluding the agent's first grab. "The note says, 'This is just a warning.'"

There was some sigh of relief, but Herman seemed frantic and yelled, "Let the dogs sniff around the house inside and out."

One of the bomb dogs scratched and whimpered at the basement door. Johnson frantically worried there was a bomb down there, but then he heard Tabby hissing back. Several concerned officers started laughing. "Josie, you can come up now. But Tabby may want to stay down there," Johnson said lightheartedly.

⌐

After all the press about the bomb scare, they pulled Josie from school for over a week until she pleaded to return.

They made secret arrangements to get her to and from school and made everyone in the class sign an agreement that they were not suppose to talk to anyone about Josie being in school.

On her first day back Josie immediately took off her shoes and started painting the bottoms to make prints when Mrs. Clemens hurried over.

"Josie what are you going to wear home if you have paint all over your shoes?"

"Oh," Josie looked at the bottoms like she hadn't thought about that. "I'll run to the car in my socks." Josie wasn't a big fan of shoes. Once fresh green grass sprung up, she was barefoot most days.

"It's winter, Josie. And there is snow on the ground."

Josie didn't remember seeing any fresh snow with all of the commotion. But then she remembered the plow mounds in parking lots still hadn't melted. "Oh. Okay I'll clean them off in the bathroom."

"Try not to make too big of a mess in there, Josie," Mrs. Clemens said shaking her head as she watched Josie turn the corner down the hall to the girls' bathroom with an officer following close behind.

Josie never returned from the bathroom. It had only been about thirty minutes since the strategic drop off. The police and news crews swarmed the grade school when the police scanners started reporting Herman's little girl was missing. Mrs. Clemens gave a statement to the police man-ically going over the details of Josie's trip to the bathroom and how she hadn't returned. Mrs. Clemens was in tears. The principal, Mrs. Dillwood, was all business and tried to place blame on the cop who was assigned to watch Josie at school. He presumably had gone to the boys' bathroom at the same time and waited down the hall within sight of the girls' bathroom for over fifteen minutes before alerting Mrs. Clemens.

Herman heard all of the reports and frantic guessing on the police radio in his car. He flipped to channel 2 and dispatch to have someone pick up his wife at the hospital and take her home. His mind was racing. He couldn't calm down. So he tried to pretend it was a case and tried not to make it personal. Pausing, frozen unable to take action, he suddenly remembered cops were already assigned and in route to pick up Jacob Williams, the suspect, who they had identified based on Josie's sketch, in the babysitter murder. So he headed over there.

Special Forces were outside the suspect's house planning for what might be a hostile arrest when Herman pulled up sirens blaring. "Wait! I think he has Josie in there!"

"We need to get in there as soon as possible then, Herman. He isn't stable," the lead officer said. Herman didn't disagree. He tried to join the arrest team but was told to stay back.

The team busted down the door, swept the rooms and found the suspect, Jacob Williams, trying to escape out a side window. As the cops pulled him back in, Jacob squealed, "I didn't hurt that girl."

"Which girl?" two officers said in unison.

"The one on TV. I didn't touch her."

"Where is she?"

"I don't know."

⌣

Jacob Williams had not kidnapped Josie. It was a woman in a dress who took her from the school bathroom. She held a chloroform-filled cloth to Josie's nose and mouth when she emerged from the bathroom stall.

Josie was blindfolded and her hands were bound in front when she woke up. Her heart was beating so fast and she could barely breathe. Several times she had imagined being kidnapped, but it was always more fun in her mind. She started to shake.

Awkwardly using her bound hands, Josie was able to lift up her blindfold, but it was pitch black. She desperately wanted her flashlight. She wondered did she know I was afraid of the dark? Was this part of her plan, to torture me? She started feeling the walls. They were brick and rough. The floor was cement, cold, and damp. Was this the same place that girl curled up like a cat was killed? But they caught that killer, I thought. Do all killers have places like this? Shouldn't places like this be outlawed then, or searched on a random basis? Josie's fear was building as horrible thoughts tumbled, one after another, through her mind.

What was it that dad taught me about tracing your surroundings if you're kidnapped? Convinced they had

had that conversation, Josie tried to remember their plan. Something about using all your senses. What did it smell like? Josie paused and tried to sniff. But her nose still seemed to be stuffed up with that nasty smell she remembered from the bathroom. She was getting frustrated. She couldn't smell or hear anything else to help her know where she was or who took her. Fear was blocking her ability to stay in the moment — thoughts of murder rushed back in. She kept thinking about how this would all turn out instead of what was happening right at that moment. She wanted to remember what was happening for later when the cops asked her questions.

She thought about curling up on the floor, but all she could envision was her own body dead like that cat-woman. But then she remembered that woman was naked. Josie let out a sigh of relief, thankful that she was still clothed. Josie wondered why she wore this silly dress and tights today. She needed to start dressing more practically if she was going to solve crimes. All of her dresses had to go, she thought. Josie ripped a strip of fine lace from her hem and pulled it apart into two strips. She looped one short piece around her ear so a small section dangled. The lace hung gently tickling her neck. Then she placed the other piece over her other ear. She wanted to know what it felt like to wear dangling earrings like Yvonne's mom did. She imagined what twenty might feel like. She hoped she would make it to twenty. She wanted to be grownup, wear grownup things, and travel on airplanes. Day dreaming about plane rides, she was able to let go of some fear of the floor and darkness, and decided to sit down on the cement with her back straight up against the wall. She closed her eyes.

"Wait! Who knew I was at school? We snuck out my backdoor, went in the back of school and I never went outside for recess. This must be a cop! Only cops knew where I was, them and everyone in my class, but no one left for the day. But I don't think anyone in my class has a killer mother. A female cop would know where this place is and they'd know it would freak me out." Josie said all of this out loud. Then covered her mouth and thought what if she is listening? Josie sat silent, trying to hear any sounds around her. She remembered hearing a muffled police radio before she woke up on the cement floor. She tried to remember more and started getting sleepy in all the darkness.

## Sparrow Street

Martha was staring at the TV set wondering why she gave the news that photo of Josie in short pigtails and a handmade dress. She seemed so much more grownup now with her hair long, past her shoulders. All of her dresses seemed short because she was growing so fast.

When Herman arrived home it seemed like half the State Police force was in the house. Some came and went but the majority stayed, waiting for the ransom call. Herman sat holding his wife for a bit. Martha held in her sobs. Herman was shaking nervously and denied it when Martha noticed.

Aunt Caroline rushed through the door when she saw all the cop cars in the driveway. "What is happening? Who is dead?"

"Who are you ma'am?" one of the plainclothes officers asked.

"Who are you? Why are you asking me questions? I did nothing wrong. Did you do something wrong? Is that why all of these cops are here?"

"I am an officer, ma'am, now will you please tell me your name and your relationship to this house?

"This house! I have no relationship with this house. I am Martha's sister. Where is Martha? Martha!"

———

From across the dining room where Herman and Martha were talking, Martha turned her back towards her sister's yelling. "I can't deal with her too. She will make this all about her." Martha said to Herman. "Can you take care of her?"

"I will." Herman gently nudged Martha towards the stairs. "You go upstairs."

"Be kind to her. She is just scared." Martha said almost in a whisper.

"Caroline, you need to calm down. These men have work to do. They are helping us find Josie." Herman said in the most patient tone he could muster at that moment.

"Josie is missing? She is always up to something. She never follows directions."

"I know. Thank you for stopping by. We'll let you know when we find her."

"I can help look?"

"Of course, why don't you check all of your closets in your house. She used to hide in them when she was really little. Remember?"

"Okay, I'll get the girls, and we'll make a game of it."

Herman shook his head as Caroline walked out the back door.

"Now that that's over! Listen guys, there isn't going to be a ransom call. We need to search!" Herman said with authority and anger.

"Herman, we don't know where to start."

"Unsolved cases. Who are we looking at for murder?" Herman said as if the idea just flashed into his mind.

"Okay, I'll pull the case files and come back," one detective said.

"A few of you guys get in your cars and search known abandoned buildings outside of the Township and the outlying woods on the other side of town. I feel like this guy is local," Post Lieutenant Michael Gray said.

"We need to put out a statement that Josie's dreams are fake. That she did the sketch from an arrest photo she found in my briefcase. That she doesn't have any special powers. If she doesn't have special powers then there's no reason to hurt her," Herman said choking on the word 'hurt.'

"Great idea, Herman," Linda said. "I'll draft a statement and read it to the press. I may have to blame you a bit for bringing home police reports."

"Blame away. My wife would agree with you that I shouldn't have it in the house," Herman said as he headed back upstairs to tell Martha what was happening.

Herman found Martha pacing around Josie's room, fiddling with Josie's collection of stuffed animals tucked in every corner of her room, and he gently coaxed her into their bedroom. "How did this happen? I told you she shouldn't go to school. This is all your fault," Martha said while crying.

"Martha, we'll find her. This must be someone we know."

"What? Someone we know? It was all over the news. It could be anybody."

"But not *anybody* knew she was at school. The media never left the front lawn. They thought she was in the house." Herman paused. "This is a cop!" Herman said as if he had just come to the conclusion at that moment.

"What?" Martha looked terrified.

"Someone on the force leaked the sketch and now they took her. There is a killer working for the State Police." Herman was getting angry.

"What?"

"There has been this weird tension at work ever since I got that recognition for the footprint case. I think they don't like how smart I am. They're worried I'll catch them. And now that I'm pushing for this promotion it has gotten worse.

I think someone wants to get me to quit. And they are trying to scare me by taking Josie."

"What are we going to do? They could be downstairs." Martha was trembling.

"You're going to stay in here with the door locked and don't open it for anyone but me. There is a gun in the closet; it's in the locked box all the way on the top shelf to the left. The key is in my sock drawer. It's loaded, be careful."

"What? You said we'd never have guns in the house. And loaded. Jesus, Herman. What if Josie found it?" Martha took a deep breath. "I can't shoot anyone."

"You can if they're going to shoot you."

"What about you?"

"I'm going to go search for Josie. Some ideas popped up about where she might be."

"Alone?"

"I'll take Anthony, he can't be the kidnapper. He was at school with her. I'm going to pretend I'm fed up and mad, demand Anthony come with me, storm out, and take a trooper's car since mine is blocked in. Lieutenant Gray will understand. He can't be the killer either. The killer will want to know where I am. And will come looking for me. This is about me in some way, I can just feel it."

"Jesus, Herman. I don't want to lose you both."

"You haven't lost Josie. He's just using her to discredit her and me. He knew I would *never* use her again on a case after this. He thinks if I don't have Josie's psychic gift I will fail. The press will issue a statement that she doesn't have any special powers, so he isn't going to hurt her." Herman wasn't sure he convinced her that Josie was going to be fine. Martha looked terrified.

"This is all too crazy. Why is this happening to us?" Martha started to cry.

"You need to be strong, Martha. Josie will need you when she returns. She'll be too terrified to use her gift. She'll need your help to try and be normal again. Everything will be okay. Soon we'll have back our sweet, cuddly girl again."

"Okay, I'll try. You be careful. And find our little girl." Martha said in an almost mute voice. Herman retrieved a gun from the locked bedside table drawer.

"Another gun? You said you hate guns."

"I do." Herman kissed his wife and tucked the gun in the back of his pants.

# 8

After stopping at the house where the babysitter was murdered — and looking in all the windows (there was no sign of any recent activity in that house, probably none since the night of the murder) — Herman drove north, fast with the sirens blaring. Anthony didn't say much. Herman had only said, "I have a hunch she's at one of the recent dumpsites. We'll go all the way to Rust if we have too." Herman turned off the police radio — all the chatter about Josie was giving him the shakes. He checked the gas gauge and thought they could make it to Owosso without stopping. He wanted to search the pine forest where they had found the woman who had been shot three times.

Once they arrived at the woods, Anthony and Herman split up and combed a wide area in opposite directions. When they met up again, Anthony said, "There is nowhere to hide her here. I see no sign of anyone even sneaking a peek at the old dump spot. The shed is a better bet."

"I agree." Herman said. They hopped back in the car, no sirens this time. Anthony seemed nervous there might be a confrontation and said they should go in silence. Herman didn't disagree. When they arrived Anthony took the back and Herman took the front door.

Josie heard crunching footsteps outside. "She's back," she whispered. Josie sat in terror and hoped she hadn't come back to remove her clothes.

Herman slowly undid the wedged latch and cracked opened the door. The light blinded Josie, but Herman saw her squinting trying to see.

"Josie!"

"Dad!" Josie ran and jumped into his arms.

"Everything is fine now. You're safe," Herman said as Josie sobbed.

Anthony came around the corner, tucking his gun away. Josie flinched when she saw him. "It's okay Josie. It's just me, Anthony. I'm so sorry this happened. I won't let you out of my sight next time."

"This is over Anthony. There'll be no next time." Herman said firmly.

"I knew you'd find me, Dad. How'd you do it?" Josie said as she climbed down from her father's arms wiping her nose on her arm.

Herman bent down to talk with her eye to eye. "I guess you're not the only one with special powers. I figured out it had to be a cop who wanted to scare you, so you would stop having your dreams and scare me, so I wouldn't use your drawings for any more cases."

"So it *is* a cop! I knew it! I thought I heard the mumbles of a police radio," she said and then frowned looking at Anthony who was in a full uniform. "I just can't see who it was."

"That's okay, Josie. Let's get you home and in a warm place. I want you to forget all about this. Let it all go. Let the lieutenant find him. I won't let this ever happen again."

"Josie what happened to your dress?" Anthony inquired in a work tone. He looked at Herman, whose face had turned ghostly, and he looked nauseous.

Josie released her clenched fist holding the lace and put the separate strips to her earlobes. "I made earrings."

The three of them laughed with relief. "That's my special girl, always creating." Herman said with a big smile.

Josie looked around as they went towards the trooper car. She thought it didn't look so scary now. She knew there were pine trees. Earlier she had started to get her sense of smell back, and now she looked up each trunk slowly as if she knew them personally. Her dad didn't hurry her along, but let her get adjusted to the light.

Josie was exhausted, still shaking from the chill and fear. She curled up in the back seat like a cat and asked, "Can we turn the sirens on?" Anthony took off his vest and put it over her. He thought maybe the weight of it would be comforting.

"Of course. But first I need to call in that we found you." Herman radioed in and reported that he and Anthony had found Josie safe and unharmed. Herman could hear a cheer in the background as Lieutenant Gray said, "That's great news, Herman!" Martha came down stairs unarmed after she heard the cheering.

Despite having questions about which cop Herman thought it might be, Anthony was quiet in the car. After he bought gas even though Josie was sound asleep, Herman flipped on the sirens and sped safely back to Martha.

Herman cut the sirens, as he neared home. Anthony radioed that they were close and that Josie was asleep. Herman didn't want to be hounded by press and wanted them to make room for the car to pull in close to the house. Martha insisted on moving her own car. She had been feeling helpless doing nothing but waiting. Once she parked the car out on the street, she scowled and shook her head at the reporters yelling, trying to ask her questions. In Martha's mind it was their fault Josie went missing. If they hadn't reported how special her little girl was, this never would have happened.

Moments later, Herman pulled into the driveway. Martha burst into tears as Herman lifted Josie from the back seat.

"Is she hurt?" Martha asked between sobs.

"No, exhausted and cold," Herman whispered.

Anthony held the door for them, and Herman carried Josie straight upstairs — she had barely stirred, but whispered "Mom" and shut her eyes again as Martha tucked her under the covers. Martha curled up in bed with her and gently drew imaginary pictures on Josie's back with her fingertips until she too fell asleep from exhaustion.

———

Lieutenant Gray was pacing at the bottom of the stairs waiting for Herman. The other officers gave him room. He was a short man and had a mean temper. He was known in his years as a cop, as the one who would beat the shit out of a suspect if needed. Though Herman wasn't afraid of him, because they had played basketball together in high school. Gray was a great guard. Since even in high school Herman stood over six feet, he usually did a lot of screening for Gray, who could power through for a layup. After reluctantly leaving Martha and Josie, Herman met him at the bottom of the stairs. Herman towered over him but slumped down humbly.

"Did the bastard hurt her at all?" Lieutenant Gray barked.

"No. She seems fine, just shaken up a bit."

"Where'd you find her?"

"Owasso, where that murdered woman was held captive."

"How'd you know she'd be there?" the lieutenant looked confused.

"We checked a few recent murder sites. We were headed to Rust next. I think it's someone on the force. Josie does too. I figured he's playing games and trying to discredit her psychic powers and picked a spot she had drawn."

"Why does he need to discredit... oh he's afraid Josie will dream about a murder he has committed?"

"Exactly. He thinks this will scare her so much she won't want to draw." Herman said a bit too loudly, and he looked over his shoulder to see who was listening.

"Shit. Let's keep this between us. Do we need to send a team up to that shed to fingerprint?"

"Wouldn't be a bad idea. But if it's a cop, I'm sure he didn't leave a single one. Though it may shake him up in some way."

"Okay, who do you want on your door tonight? I can stay," the lieutenant offered.

"No, you go home to your family. Anthony and Johnson seem to be a safe bet."

"Okay, done."

"So he didn't touch her, right?"

"Her clothing looked unruffled, minus the lace she tore off herself. And she would have told us if the son-of-a-bitch touched her. He did take her somewhere that would terrify her. Left her in the dark and inside of the same shed she drew with the murdered girl in it. He apparently left her there with a flimsy stick wedging the door closed. Not sure he was coming back."

"Arrogant bastard!"

"I'm glad he doesn't have the stomach to kill little girls. He must only kill women."

"Me too, Herman. So we're looking for someone on the force with children, is my guess. We'll find him. We'll find him." The lieutenant mumbled it the second time he said it as he walked away to round up the officers to clear out the house and let Johnson and Anthony know they were on the doors.

The next day Herman stayed home, though he wanted to get back to the Lab and work on the babysitter case. Work always settled the stress for him, or so he told himself. Martha was fussing over Josie, making all of her favorite foods and stuffing her with forbidden sugar. Herman sat motionless in his favorite chair and Josie sprawled out on the floor, resting in the sun, and chattered on about every detail she heard in the shed.

"There was a woman I had never seen before in the bathroom. But I only saw her for less than a second in the mirror before I went into the stall. Then I don't remember anything about coming out of the stall, it all goes black. I smelled something funny when I was peeing."

"Herman, shouldn't you be writing this all down?" Martha interrupted from the kitchen.

"The lieutenant will need to do all that. We're just giving her some time to recover a bit. Go on, Josie."

Josie talked until she fell asleep on the floor and Herman carried her upstairs. When Herman came down, and he told Martha he was going to the Lab for a bit. Martha protested but not too strongly. She too was exhausted and went upstairs to cuddle with Josie.

Herman was greeted nearly at the door by a few of his co-workers, who immediately sent him back home. He complied, but took a few reports with him to catch up on the babysitter case.

The next day, the Banks family tried to find some normalcy in their routine. Martha went to the front door to grab the morning paper, and she let out a frightening scream. Herman and Johnson ran out front. Josie followed, but Johnson and Herman, at the same time, yelled, "Josie, down in the basement, now."

After Josie heard laughter, she let herself out of the basement figuring they had forgotten she was down there and all of the danger had passed. She crept up to the front door where she could see her mom was scrubbing the bricks. In large capital letter, someone had spray painted "liar" on the front of the house.

"Dad, I don't lie. Grandma always told me that if I lied it would come back in my carmom." Josie said.

Herman chuckled, "You mean karma."

"Josie this is not about you," Martha quickly jumped in before Herman said anything else. "I know you don't lie. Herman finish scrubbing this." Martha handed him the brush. Herman looked perplex. "I'm going to fix Josie breakfast."

## The Lab

Sneaking out early the next day, Herman arrived at the Bridgeport Lab through the driveway between the Bridgeport Post and the Lab (passing the common gas pump). The Michigan State Police runs on gas. With the current oil embargo there were several occasions when the State Police simply parked their patrol cars ("Blue Goose's") in the median of the nearby freeway hoping to slow the traffic. They had no gas to chase down speeders.

Herman made his way past the friendly officer at the front door where the secretary normally played a tough gatekeeper. After he checked his desk for any messages he went further down the main hall on the left to the trace evidence laboratory, the Microchemical Unit. He sat down at one of the smaller benches along the side supporting microscopes. The room also had two large empty tables in the center of the room covered in clothing that needed to be searched for blood and trace evidence.

Herman finished up the microscopical testing, which demonstrated an abundance of intact human spermatozoa in the babysitter's vagina. The genetic markers matched the markers in a semen stain on the outside of the fly area of Jacob's underwear. Two pubic hairs found on Karen's sweater and one on her plaid skirt were similar in all respects to Jacob's pubic hair. The hair on her sock was similar to Jacob's head hair. A search of Jacob's shoes revealed a crusted red-brown stain on the outside edge of the left shoe sole, near the toe, which matched the genetic markers of the babysitter's blood.

"Herman, what you doing here?" Lieutenant Gray said with concern. "I thought I told you to take a few days."

"You did, sir, but lab work helps relax my nerves. Any leads on Josie's kidnapper?"

"Not yet. I have internal affairs looped in," the lieutenant whispered. "The FBI has been looking into the case as well. They seem pretty interested in Josie's dreams."

"Sure, do they need to talk to Josie or me?"

"Not yet. We'll get Josie in here soon, and if we can I'd like her to walk around a bit to see if anyone shies away from talking to her."

"Okay, I'm sure she'd be up for that. She would probably go desk-to-desk if she had it her way. She doesn't play small. Nearly fearless if she has a flashlight. But I'll tell her she has to make more of a game of it."

"She is special. I'm sure the FBI will want to talk to her one-on-one at some point too, if you and Martha don't mind."

"I'm fine with that. We'll see if Martha will go for it. She seems suspicious of all cops now, well, besides Johnson and Anthony."

"Okay, let me know. I have to run, morning meetings. There's always meetings. You get home soon."

"Will do, sir."

Herman went back to work and used lifting tape to collect foreign fibers from the babysitter's and Jacob's clothing, which had been bagged as evidence at the scene and collected upon Jacob's arrest. Jacob's coat lining was littered with an abundance of yellow alpaca wool fibers. Likewise, numerous bright yellow alpaca fibers were found on his red shirt. Similar alpaca fibers were found on the babysitter's sweater. As part of a cross transfer, several white acrylic fibers, similar to the white acrylic fibers from babysitter's white sweater, and a polyester fiber similar to polyester fibers from her torn brassiere, were recovered from Jacob's red shirt.

After finding the alpaca fibers, Herman went over to the Post and marched swiftly through the questions abo' how Josie was, and found the lead detective on the case, "There must be a yellow sweater or blanket out there." Herman blurted out.

"Okay, Herman. We'll get someone out to Jacob's place tomorrow. Now you stop worrying about this case and take care of Josie."

Herman nodded, put his coat on, walked head down back through the officers, and headed home.

## Sparrow Street

Herman came home to a house full of people, casseroles, and familiar faces but some forgotten names, just like after his mother's funeral. Martha looked a bit overwhelmed, but Josie loved it. She was telling each person a full detailed report about what had happened. Sharpening her memory, she called it, though she did this against her dad's wishes that she would let it go. There was a missing piece. She couldn't figure it out yet. She thought if she went through it out over and over, it would come back to her.

"I was in the bathroom stall, and I heard someone with heavy feet enter the stall next to me. Then I opened the latch and as I was headed to wash my hands..." One little old lady interrupted and said, "It's good that you wash your hands after you use the bathroom. My granddaughter does not." Josie didn't miss a beat. "Then I felt a hand reach around my face. Then. Nothing!" One woman gasped. "Everything is black after that. No dreams. Just nothing."

"Josie, you may be scaring some of the guests," Herman said gently.

"Oh. Am I?" Josie looked around at the concerned faces.

"Well, maybe reliving it so many times is not best, Josie," her Aunt Caroline said.

"And it's getting late," Herman said with a nudge, pointing Josie towards the stairs. Josie started to cry. "What is it?" Herman sounded concerned.

"She pushed me like that."

"Okay, I won't do that again. I think it's time for you to get some rest."

Martha instinctively put her body in between Herman and Josie. She picked up Josie with a strain, but Josie held on tight as they went up the stairs.

"Your dad didn't mean to scare you. I'm so sorry you had to go through all of this. Sweet Josie, you *will* be fine." Martha said as she laid Josie in bed and then kissed her forehead.

Josie turned over, faced the wall and curled up with her flashlight and Tabby. A rotten feeling came over Josie, like the kidnapper was in the room. She wondered if it was one of the cops at the house. One was different from yesterday.

"Dad!" Josie yelled after her mom left the room. "Dad!"

Martha and Herman came running, "What is it, Josie?" Herman said as Martha listened by the door.

"I want those cops out of the house. They're making me feel funny."

"Well, you know Johnson, Jo. I'm going to have him stay, but I will send home Edwards. He's new. Now get some rest."

"Is Edwards a killer?" Martha frantically whispered as she and Herman walked back downstairs.

Herman grabbed her arm. "Now, Martha, don't jump to conclusions. These are the men I work with. Josie is still scared from the shed, over tired, and she's had too much sugar. I'll send him home and see how he responds. Johnson is going to be beat if he is the only one she'll let protect her." Johnson and Herman went to grade school together. He was about the only cop he emphatically trusted besides Lieutenant Gray. Martha really didn't trust Gray or Johnson, but the sports bond was tight between them, so she kept her mouth shut. Martha sent everyone home at that point — she worried how it would appear just sending Edwards home. Though appearances were getting harder and harder to keep up with.

⌐

Josie woke up in the middle of the night and lurched to a seated position in her bed. She hadn't had a dream or one she could remember, but she had a huge urge to draw. She turned on her flashlight, took out her paper and paint, and drew an outline of the shed. This time her painting was messy, and almost lacked straight lines, and she didn't use realistic colors. She wondered if her powers were going away. Who was it her grandmother used to quote? Josie thought. Someone named Marianne Williamson. I don't know her, but my grandmother must have. Anyways she used to say to me, "You are a child of God. You are meant to shine. Your playing small doesn't serve the world. You are powerful beyond measure." Josie didn't feel like she was shining at that moment, more lost because she couldn't see the woman who took her no matter how hard she tried. The shed drawing was full of emotion now. She painted it wild and enormous. Nothing Josie did was small. She liked to think big thoughts, paint big pictures, climb to the highest branch, and had a piercing loud scream that could wake the neighbors. About the only thing she did small was her doodling. Tiny scenes that from a distance might even look like flowers but in fact were crime scenes. Tiny human faces drawn with just a few lines. But this night she painted larger than life images.

The next morning, entering Josie's room while her daughter was still asleep, Martha gasped at the mess Josie had created in her bed. Josie stirred and said, "What's wrong, Mom?"

"What happened last night?"

Josie pushed the covers back and her drawing and paints fell to the floor. "I woke up and painted, but I must have fallen back asleep. I'm sorry, Mom." Josie started to cry.

"It's okay, sweetheart." Martha hugged Josie. "Maybe just pencils and paper up here, and we can leave the painting supplies downstairs. How's that sound?"

"Okay."

"What did you paint here?" Martha couldn't make out that it was the shed. It was red and deep purple, and lacked a sure shape.

"The shed."

"Oh, I see now." Martha could only see fire and pain and asked if she could take this one to work with her. Josie didn't acknowledge her request. She didn't see how it would help anything this time. Martha wanted to show this one to the hospital's resident psychiatrist.

## The Lab

The detectives went to Jacob's wife and asked about the yellow fibers Herman had found. His wife, Brenda, pointed to a yellow sweater over in the corner and said, "Jacob wore that the night of the murder." The officers bagged it up and took it back to the Lab for testing.

Jacob claimed to have an alibi. Nevertheless, he was charged with murder and Herman's department was pretty convinced they would get a conviction despite some concern over a faulty search warrant for blood, saliva, and hair samples from the defendant. They had many other incriminating comparisons including the yellow sweater match, and the little girl as a witness — who was so traumatized she could only really confirm she saw Jacob in the house before she went to bed. But because of the nature of her trauma, the psychologist suspected she had witnessed the whole murder from the upstairs balcony. All of this established that the defendant was the last known person to be at the scene before the killing. Herman was confident Josie's drawings wouldn't even have to come up.

# 9

About a week later after Josie had indulged in even more special treatment, including Tupperwares full of cookies again, Martha found Josie surrounded by a stack of drawings of Herman.

"Have you been up all night, Josie?" Martha said in concerned voice.

"I don't think so." Josie didn't look up from what she was drawing.

"There are so many drawings here, you must've been." Martha started thumbing through them.

"Do you like them? I was trying to make one for your birthday, but I don't think I have it quite right yet." Josie started looking through them too.

"They're lovely. You pick your favorite and I'll frame it."

"Okay, but I want to try a few more." Josie started drawing again.

"Well, you need to get ready for school now," Martha said in a mothering tone.

"I'm not feeling well. Can I stay home again today?" Josie pleaded.

"What's wrong?" Martha put her wrist on Josie's forehead. "You don't seem to have a fever."

"It's my stomach. It hurts."

Martha tried to convince Josie that maybe breakfast would help and then maybe she could go to school. Josie didn't budge. She held firm that she was sick. Martha finally gave in and brought up ginger ale and some soda crackers in case she was hungry.

———

"What kind of sick is she?" Herman asked after he inquired if Josie was coming down for breakfast. He had already filled her bowl with cereal. Josie liked to eat whatever cereal her dad was having. Sometimes he ate the frosted kind. Josie had learned even though she wasn't allowed kids' cereal, the grownup stuff had lots of sugar too. Therefore she played along with the Bran Flakes until his cereal rotation made it to Frosted Mini Wheats, when she always asked for seconds.

"It's her stomach," Martha mumbled.

"She can't be missing any more school," Herman said argumentatively.

"I tried! What do you want me to do? She seems upset, and her stomach is bothering her. I'm not going to force the issue. She's been through so much."

"So now she's feeling upset? I thought it was just her stomach?"

"Well it's not the flu — she doesn't have a fever. I don't think that peanut butter and jelly she ate for dinner gave her food poisoning." Martha's voice began to get louder. "So I figured it's probably emotional trauma of some sort. You know like normal people have after they see...what she's seen."

"Oh, you had to get a dig in about my work. You sound just like my mother. Blaming my work for everything. Couldn't think maybe it was the kidnapping that is upsetting her?"

"Isn't that related to work too? You said you thought it was probably a cop that took her. Can't you find another line of work? Why do you have to bring all of this violence into our lives?"

"I'm doing this to protect Josie. I'm doing this to help protect you both. I want to make the world safer for Josie to grow up in. I want less of these murders out there so there is less of a chance they'll hurt her."

"But her dreams won't stop, and now she's drawing you over and over. How are you helping her at this point? Look at her now."

Josie could clearly hear the fight with her ear pressed against the metal air vent on the floor. She wondered if "now" meant they would be coming upstairs, and she should pretend to be doing something.

"Maybe we can get her some help, send her to a therapist. Maybe they can teach her how to stop the dreams."

"Now you want to send her because she's drawing pictures of you and not helping your cases. You were using her."

"Martha, you're being absurd!" Herman took a deep breath. "I'll ask around the station and see if anyone recommends a psychologist that deals with violence issues."

"I'll have no state doctor come anywhere near her. I'll find someone through the hospital." Martha walked off and went upstairs to check on Josie, a new habit after each fight. She started asking Josie what she heard and if she wanted to talk about any of it. Josie usually didn't know how to respond, but this time she asked what a psychologist would do to her. Martha had to explain that you just talked and a psychologist would help Josie's mind not to see such scary stuff. Josie was skeptical. She didn't want anyone tampering with her dreams. She started trying to figure out a plan to keep the doctor out of her mind.

The phone rang, Herman answered and then he left the house without saying goodbye. Martha let out a heavy huff when she heard the door close. "You going to be okay by yourself today, Josie?"

"I'll be fine. Just going to stay up here."

"I'll try to come home early and make you some soup. And I'll have your aunt stop by a few times. Johnson is by the door or in the kitchen."

"That's fine." Josie had already gone back to drawing.

## The Lab

Herman packed up the state car with fresh supplies before the other examiners arrived — Sergeant Greg Adams and Dean Madison helped once they rolled in. It was an unusual time to be heading out to a scene — right before business hours. All of them were feeling flustered like they were late though the crime scene was close by in Bay City.

Reports indicated that Mark Baldwin had returned home from his night shift to find the partially clad body of his wife, Patricia, stabbed and mutilated in their home. A fresh fallen snow lay on top of the other eight inches already on the ground that morning as the crime scene investigators arrived. Her body was by the back door — lying on the floor right in the kitchen doorframe. Her leg was sticking out the door and prevented it from closing. "Anyone come through this door since the murder?" Herman asked. A cop standing guard replied, "No, sir," with a military tone. Herman twirled around and directed Greg and Dean to walk back around the house and enter through the front. They were just about to do that anyway. They said, "Yes, sir!" in the same military tone and walked off. Herman was feeling the stress from home and the unsolved cases were piling up.

This case was the start of a week that would include a thirty-six-hour workday for the Bridgeport Lab examiners and an investigation hinged on evidence as small as a single hair, as fragile as a palmprint on wallpaper and as obscure as the impression of one fabric on another. With no leads and a half-dressed victim, this case was feeling familiar to Herman.

"This one's odd to me. He just jumped her right in the heat of the moment. Steps over her to exit, but did not notice the door didn't close. Some killers are not so bright," Herman said to Dean as the coroner put her in a body bag.

Dean nodded. "I hate to say it, but the string of murders lately all have a similar feel to them."

"I was just thinking the same thing. Well, maybe someone needs to kill a man in this town to even things out. Remember the crispy critter case?"

"How could you forget, every state Lab seem to show up at the crime scene. You couldn't even tell it was a man, the pathologist had to determine that by his pelvis. Our Lab was taking bets it was a woman. Maybe we should take bets that the next one is a man," Dean said.

"Yeah, but it can't be just a drug dealer or junky. Just some prick," said Herman. He thought Josie never had dreams about junkies being killed. Nor had any of her dreams involved a man being killed. There was a link here of some sort that he wanted to figure out. He wished his mother were still alive; maybe she would have some answers.

"I'm with you. Just some random dude. We don't need another crispy critter case. We'll have to wait and see. As much as my wife would like crimes to happen between the hours of nine and five, so she could sleep, I have a feeling we are due for a weekend murder." Dean said as he finished packing up from the crime scene.

Soon thereafter, a police spokesman reported the crime laboratory had apparently found very few clues. The press quizzed the spokesman as to whether Josie would help on this case.

"Josie is recovering from her kidnapping and will no longer be consulting on any cases," the spokesman said firmly.

Herman was a bit sad when he overheard the spokesman standing outside the crime scene as they packed up the wagon. She has a gift, he thought. His mother would want her to use it. And he needed a hint here; this case looked like it could turn cold. No one knew on that early morning that there was a valuable clue yet to be discovered.

Herman came home early to check on Josie. He found her upstairs with cigarette butts, knives, rope, a ladder, leaves, and ties like her kidnapper used to restrain her.

"Josie, what is all this?" Herman looked concerned. "You shouldn't have these knives." Herman picked them up.

Josie was drawing a fragmented looking portrait.

"Josie, look at me. Are you working on the case I got called on this morning?"

"Do you want it for your desk?" Josie hadn't heard his question she was still focused on drawing.

"What do you mean, Josie? Is this a new murderer you've seen in your dreams?"

"No, Dad. It's you. Can't you see that?"

"Oh, now I see it. I was looking upside down at it, Jo." Herman looked around at all the portraits on the floor. They were all him. The ones on top were increasingly more abstract. "Why don't you take a break? Let's take Tabby for a walk. Come on." Josie slowly followed her father around the block a few paces back, watching Tabby closely, afraid she'd run away. Herman was annoyed with her pace. He turned around at one point and said, "Maybe we should go back the faster way through the field if you are tired." Josie shook her head no and her father noticed fear in her eyes but didn't say anything. Her mother was pulling in the driveway when they rounded the corner close to the house. Josie cheered up a bit when she saw her mom. She even put Tabby down to help her mom with the groceries. Herman disappeared.

Martha told Josie to go up to bed after several lazy hours on the soft new couch. When she entered her dark room and flicked on the light she saw that all of her "evidence" and drawings were gone. She looked frantically under her bed for any trace of her work. "Even my flashlight is gone!" Josie yelled. Her mother was frightened by the pitch of Josie's voice and came running upstairs from the kitchen.

Johnson was on Martha's heels. She turned to him, "I got this."

Josie screamed and accused her mother of taking her things. Her mother pleaded, "Why would I take your flashlight. I bought it for you. Josie, please calm down. I didn't take your things."

Josie stormed past her and yelled down the stairs to Johnson, who was standing on the bottom step eager to go up to help. "Did you hear anyone sneak in the front door?" He shook his head no. She yelled out to her mom, "We need two men, one on the front door too!"

"Josie you need to calm down. I'll get you another flashlight." Martha pleaded.

"It's not about the flashlight. Someone thinks I know too much." Josie sat and cried. She had a suspicion her father had taken everything but didn't tell anyone.

Once Martha got Josie calmed down and tucked her into bed, she grilled Johnson about where Herman was.

"He's on a case. It just came in. A man was found dead. He was hung similar to the woman down the block at the barn. He was the only one called in, since it looks like just a 907 — I mean a suicide. They never call out the whole team for those but since it looked too similar to the barn case, well that's why they sent Herman. That's all I can tell you. I shouldn't have even told you that much." Johnson looked a bit overwhelmed.

"Thank you, Johnson. I appreciate your honesty. There's so much stress in this house. It's hard to know the facts of what is really going on around here. What is happening in this town? All this violence!"

"It comes in waves. This too shall pass. It always does."

# 10

After Josie's latest outburst when her drawing materials went missing, Martha made attempts to distract Josie from focusing on her dreams. She thought maybe getting a dog would help, but Tabby was in a panic as soon as the dog showed up, and she began shedding large clumps of fur. The new pet had to go back only a few days later. Jose was so upset about Tabby going bald that she didn't even notice the dog was gone. Josie collected all of Tabby's clumps of fur and put them in a tiny wicker basket, which she hid up in the attic.

The next week, Martha signed Josie up for a dance class, but Josie complained she didn't fit in and hated wearing her hair in a bun. She preferred it long and wild, never brushed, which was forbidden in ballet class. Martha didn't push it. She hated seeing Josie so unhappy.

One afternoon right in the middle of a severe Michigan winter, when the ice and wind made outings ridiculous, Josie wanted to go for ice cream. They went to Mooney's and Josie insisted on bringing in her new scooter. She mutely rode her scooter around the parlor, squeezing in between customers and waiting for them to move their chairs so she could slide between the tables of patrons chatting and snacking. She never said a word or made eye contact with anyone. There was just an awkward stop until one of the adults made room for her to glide around. Martha watched and worried as she went around and around at a slow pace. Silently, Josie moved along — her only action was a labored push with one foot and a short glide. Even with her favorite sundae, Martha couldn't coax her away from her looping.

There were many other attempts to add activities to Josie's days, but Martha had failed to redirect Josie's attention or get to the root problem. Josie frowned while at museums or the roller rink. Martha even gave in and got Josie's ears pierced. One Saturday Martha took Josie on a road trip to see the lighthouse along the Blue Water area of Michigan's east shoreline. Jose was obsessed with the lighthouse and normally she joyfully watched the shoreline for boats and the circling light while doodling landscape drawings, which Martha would usually frame and give relatives for Christmas gifts. This trip she only demanded to get home because she forgot to bring her mother's old purse filled with paper and markers. The only thing that seemed to keep her content was more paints and paper. Josie had a gift that her parents were increasingly frightened of. And Josie had no plans of being small to make them feel more comfortable. She continued drawing the details of any of her dreams about the unsolved cases.

Martha didn't know how to help Josic. She thought her best option was to redirect her own life and let Josie work through her pain with markers. "I've been thinking about

Josie so much and ignoring you." Martha said to Herman when he arrived home late from the Lab. "I bought you something." Martha handed Herman a book wrapped in colorful pink and blue paper left over from a friend's baby shower.

Herman smirked about the paper. He meticulously removed the scotch tape, not tearing the paper. A smile appeared across his face when he saw the copy of *Invisible Cities*.

"I asked one of the doctors at work what was on the bestseller list, he said Calvino's latest. I hope you like it."

"Thank you. It's been so long since I've read fiction. This will be a treat." Herman kissed Martha sweetly and then headed to his reading chair and switching on the police scanner. He needed the quiet hum of work in the background, a habit Josie had picked up as well.

Adam and Danny finally got out of their afternoon piano lessons and were able to help Josie dig holes to hide her drawings.

"Josie, the ground is too hard," Danny proclaimed as he stuck the pointy tip of the shovel into the earth and it didn't budge."

"It's frozen." Adam chimed in.

"Okay, well we have to build better boxes if they are going to stay above ground."

"I have an idea. Let's cover them with masking tape like we did the balloons for paper mache."

"Great idea. My dad has some in the garage." Danny took off towards his house.

They sat on Adam's back porch winding the tape roll around shoeboxes, sealing the cardboard, and making the tops extra sturdy.

"They will blow away. We need rocks on the top."

They jumped on their dirt bikes and went down the block to search the woods for rocks. The boys grabbed giant ones they could barely lift.

"Guys, those will crush the boxes, and I am the one that has to lift the lids off to put stuff in. Smaller!"

Adam and Danny proudly chucked the rocks into the creek, and then gathered up stones with Josie.

They created an elaborate nest out of branches and small rocks and hid the boxes in the evergreen bushes alongside both Adam and Danny's houses. Josie said she'd stash her dad's size thirteen shoebox in the lilac bush once she knew her parents had gone to work the next morning.

"Which one is the lilac?" Danny asked.

"My favorite one. The one that flowers that I cut fresh branches for Mrs. Clemens?" The boys still looked confused. "The one down below my bedroom window."

"Oh, got it." They said nearly in unison.

⌐

After many weeks, the gray winter skies were showing signs of clearing but Martha's headaches had increased in fre-quency. Herman's preoccupation with work had grown.

"Herman, I can't handle everything on my own. You're home less and less. Josie is more confused now that you show no interest in her drawings," Martha said to Herman from across the dinner table, after Josie had silently left the table to clear her dishes. It wasn't clear if he was listening. "Did you hear me, Herman?" Martha barked with her arms crossed tightly across her body.

"Yes, Martha. I'll talk with Josie," Herman said in a somber tone without making eye contact with Martha.

Martha knew that familiar dismissive tone and couldn't contain her anger. "Your mother would be appalled at how you've been treating Josie."

"How dare you bring my mother into this. She would be disgusted at how weak you are. Complaining that you can't handle this family. She handled everything."

Martha stormed off, leaving the table uncleared and a mess in the kitchen.

———

Herman didn't have a talk with Josie. He had grown concerned about her repeatedly drawing his portrait. He avoided her even after Martha's frequent demands. If Herman was even home, his nose was in a book, usually nonfiction and something science based. Josie snuck his books into her room when he wasn't home and tried to read them. Although she really couldn't understand the science, she kept looking at the books with crime scene photos. She brought one to school for show-and-tell, which had a naked dead

woman in it. When her teacher found out, Josie was escorted to the principal's office. Josie pleaded and argued that
she didn't know the body was in there. Josie's defensiveness
didn't work this time, and she was sent home for two days.

Martha didn't say a word to Josie on the car ride home.
She was preoccupied by her anger towards Herman. Once
home Martha flew into a rage and started a bonfire of his
books in the backyard. Martha methodically tossed one
book at a time into the fire as if she were mindfully remov-
ing all the violence from her house. She had sent Josie to her
room. Though Josie had opened the window to let in the
smell of dusty burning books. It reminded her of her family's last camping trip when her grandmother was still alive.
She knew her dad was going to be furious, so she kept herself
busy cleaning her room and brushing Tabby. In the yard,
Martha's wrinkled angry brow slowly shifted to remorseful
tears as the pile grew and the fire department arrived.

The neighbors had called the fire department and they
alerted Herman that his backyard was on fire. He rushed
home to find half his books smoldering and soaked with water. Martha was standing over them head down in shame.
Herman loved his books. "I fell in love with the man who
loved to read great literature. Not the books in this pile.
There's so much death in these books. You're obsessed with
death — ever since your brother died. It's all you can think
about and now with your mother gone — well it's even
worse." Herman didn't respond or even look at Martha. He
went into the house and packed up what remained of his

books and left to take them to the Lab. Josie stayed upstairs fearful that she could cause her parents to get a divorce like the family down the street. She hoped her father was coming back. She didn't understand his distance, and she missed helping with the cases, but lately it felt like he didn't believe in her dreams.

## The Lab

The snow finally melted after a rare day of warm winter sunshine. The Department had a suspect under investigation for the murder of the woman found on her kitchen floor and half out the door. Herman and Dean went with the arrest team to facilitate the search warrant.

When the police arrived, they found a knife lying casually in the suspect's truck-bed. It appeared that the murderer ran out the victim's kitchen door to where his pickup truck was parked in the driveway with ten inches of snow in the back. He had tossed the knife, the murder weapon, in the back and headed home. This wasn't uncommon; Herman had been at other crime scenes when the murder weapon had been "stashed" almost in plain sight. The police were amused when they saw the knife.

Herman walked up to the truck carrying forensic supplies and said, "Most people don't think too clearly after butchering a woman. Crazy, sloppy killers have some sort of issue and proper disposal of the murder weapon isn't their first priority."

"Well, there's one case closed. Maybe with that murder of the man last week, this cycle will all change," Dean said as he put the knife in an evidence bag.

The officers cuffed the truck owner and read him his rights. Herman stared at the man with contempt. He was tall and broad-shouldered but had a squirrelly walk. Dean gave him a nudge. "This one get to you, Herman?"

"No." Herman said frankly. "Josie has been drawing these portraits that are rather abstract, and I was just seeing if there was any resemblance to him in them." Herman was really looking to see if this guy looked anything thing like him. If the two of them looked similar, maybe Josie had gotten confused and had drawn her father instead. Although Herman couldn't see the resemblance other than they were both Caucasian with brown hair. Maybe their eyes were a similar shape but Herman thought that was a stretch.

The murderer finally took note of Herman's gaze and yelled in his direction. "Like what you see, or what I did?" Herman looked away and didn't acknowledge the suspect as the cop yanked harder on the cuffs and moved him along.

## Sparrow Street

As mounds of snow melted, saturating the earth, the spring rains also dumped water across the middle stretch of Michigan. The sump pump clanked and banged in the basement and each time Martha heard it she jumped. She had been increasingly jittery since the kidnapping, and she had tried not to show Josie, but clearly jumping at strange noises wasn't something she could hide. Johnson offered to look at the pump to make sure it was working correctly. "Oh no, I'm sure it is working fine. Well, maybe it isn't. I can't say I've checked it. I haven't gone to the basement to do laundry since the kidnapping."

"Well that was about three weeks ago and we'd had a lot of snow melt." Johnson said trying not to sound amazed that she hadn't done laundry for so long.

"But it's late, and I'm sure your wife would love for you to come home."

"It doesn't matter. When I arrive home, she's always upset that I'm here protecting Josie, since officially they took someone off the door. I shouldn't have told her that part." Johnson shrugged and smiled. "I prefer to be here when Herman is stuck at work. I'll go take a look," Johnson said. Martha smiled and kept herself from rolling her eyes about Herman being stuck. She hovered close to the stairs while keeping Josie in sight in the dining room. A few minutes later Johnson emerged from the stairwell wet up to his knees. "It appears to be broken. Your concern was justified."

"Oh no! Where is Tabby? Her litter box is down there! Josie said she was missing, but I didn't want to deal with it. I was afraid maybe she'd lead us to another body. Now this!"

"Tabby is in the litter box and is happily floating around. She seemed nervous when I approached, so I think I'll let you get her out. We haven't quite bonded yet."

"She only loves Josie and, well, her grandmother. The rest of us are just too ordinary I guess. I really can't deal with this!" Martha sat down instead of moving into action.

"Shall I radio Herman?" Johnson asked.

"What is he going to do? He can't fix anything, and he'll just walk around hollering and complaining that everything is broken." Martha grumbled. "JOSIE! Get your boots on."

"Will you let me help too?"

"I wouldn't normally but…"

"Johnson, why are you all wet?" Josie asked when she entered the kitchen.

"Put on your boots. We have to rescue Tabby. She's floating in her litter box."

"What? A flood down there?" Josie started down the stairs while putting on her boots.

"Slow down, Josie. We have lots of work to do. I can't be taking you to the hospital for a broken arm or leg." Martha grabbed Josie's arm to stop her from descending the stairs any further. "Johnson, can you go to the garage and grab the stack of buckets?"

"Will do."

Martha released Josie. "Go slowly."

Josie waded to the back of the basement to find the litter box lodged between the furnace and water heater. The water was above the plugs.

"Wait! I need to shut off the power. Get out of the water, Josie!"

"Wait! I don't have my flashlight!"

"Go get it. I'll cut the power."

Martha waded through the water and tried to remember what the nuns at the orphanage had said about floods and turning off the power. Without a father and her mother in and out of the picture, she never learned these things. Was it don't turn it off if you are standing in water? I have on rubber boots, which means I'll be fine, right? She held her breath as she switched off basement breakers. The basement turned to complete darkness, and she was still alive. She saw the flashlight light bouncing to Josie's playful walk through the water.

⌐

Herman finally arrived home and joined the cleanup. He didn't even ask what happened and just joined in the chain of bucket passing. The three of them looked so exhausted. He felt guilty for not being there earlier. After several hours of scooping up buckets of water and pouring them down the laundry sink drain, Johnson became convinced the drain was a direct route back into the basement since they weren't making much headway. Martha called it quits. She sent Josie to bed and Johnson home.

As Martha and Herman snored, almost cuddling in bed, Josie had a dream that her dad took the rope from her room and strung up that drunk man, who supposedly had committed suicide. It was rare that Josie had new nightmares about crimes that occurred weeks ago. With all the past crimes, her dreams were always fresh on the night of the murders and normally repeated themselves. This was different. She woke up sweating and scared. She wanted to cry for help, but she couldn't tell anyone what she had seen. She was afraid to close her eyes again. She didn't want to see the image of her dad stringing up that man while he was still alive, begging under the cloth muzzle shoved into his mouth.

"Grandma you saw the future — is this why you left?" Josie whispered while crying. "I need to leave." Josie got out of bed and packed warm clothes and extra shoes into her school backpack and a gym duffle bag. She tucked them in her closet. She snuck downstairs to the kitchen and grabbed several Carnation breakfast bars, a jar of peanuts, loaf of bread, peanut butter, and one large, sharp kitchen knife. She heard footsteps upstairs and stashed the supplies in a bag in the cupboard. She took out a glass, poured some milk, in case one of her parents came downstairs. She stood silently, and when she heard the toilet flush and the footsteps stop, she downed the full glass of milk.

She searched for her mom's purse, grabbed all her cash, and then the coins from the change bowl by the door. She took the bag of groceries upstairs and tucked it into her duffel bag, then stashed the money in her backpack's front zipper pocket. Next, she got her toothbrush and a small tube of toothpaste, some toilet paper and Band-Aids then locked the knob on the bathroom door on her way out to buy herself more time. Quietly, she went to the garage and took her mother's more powerful flashlight out of the car. Back in the house, she wondered if she should write a note. She decided against it and left.

It was four a.m. and she wasn't sure where she was headed. Briskly, she walked left down the block in the opposite direction of the barn. Everything in her neighborhood looked different at night. Thankfully she remembered her grandmother's magical words, "I am safe and free." Josie repeated them silently as she walked in a familiar direction.

# 11

Martha woke up before her alarm went off and sleepily traversed to the bathroom. She had a sick feeling in her stomach and wondered what she had eaten last night. Then she wondered if that patient she cared for with a high fever had maybe given her the flu. She hoped she wouldn't pass whatever this was along to Josie. Herman was adamant that Josie shouldn't miss any more school. Moving slowly from the master bath, Martha went back to the bed and woke Herman. "Will you wake up Josie? I'm not feeling well and don't want to give whatever I might have to her."

Herman groggily nodded and slowly emerged from under the covers. Stretching and grumbling as his joints cracked, he was achy and overtired. This wasn't the first time he felt old at thirty-three. He wondered if that was why his mom had died so young. She had complained about feeling old at thirty. Similar to Herman's, her mind never rested. They were both always trying to stay one step ahead of something.

Drowsily Herman went down the hall and opened Josie's door, which was closed. Herman took note that it was odd; she normally liked the door partially open for Tabby to come and go. Herman walked in and Tabby frantically circled around his ankles. For a moment, Herman lost his footing and nearly tripped. "What is it with you cat?" Herman mumbled. "Josie," Herman shooed Tabby away and without looking at the bed. "Josie," he repeated as he looked up. Grumpily, Herman rolled his eyes and thought, now what. This must be why Martha sent me. She didn't want to hunt her down all over the house.

Then Herman went downstairs. It was pitch dark, so he switched on a few lights. No sign of Josie other than a dirty milk glass on the counter and a few open cupboards. He went to the top of the basement stairs and flicked on the light switch. "Josie, are you down there?" he hollered. No answer. He went back upstairs, realizing he hadn't even looked in the bathroom. The door was closed, and he laughed a bit to himself that he was overreacting. He figured Martha's paranoia was getting to him. He knocked on the door. No answer. "Josie, you in there? I'm coming in." With a firm hold on the doorknob, Herman pushed and his shoulder bumped into the door. The door was locked. With a closed fist, Herman started pounding. "Josie, open this door!" Martha came running out of their room.

"What is happening?"

"Josie has locked herself in here and isn't responding."

"The light is off, Herman. Maybe she's hurt or sick?"

"She hurt herself in the bathroom?" Herman said with skepticism. "She's probably locked herself in there again doing one of her 'scientific' experiments with toothpaste and mouthwash. She's playing games. She's trying to get our attention."

"Well, she has it." Martha raised her eyebrows in annoyance. "And she hasn't been playing with toothpaste for years. So let's figure out how to open that lock or break the damn thing down."

Herman slammed his right shoulder into the door while holding the knob hoping it would pop open. No luck. Martha went for a bobby pin. They tugged back and forth on the pin, while arguing over who was going to pick the lock. "Martha, you've never picked a lock. Let me try." Martha had. On the rare occasion when her mother had a home and the girls weren't being shipped around to foster homes or the Catholic orphanage, her annoying sister Caroline regularly locked herself in their shared bedroom. Martha usually had to wait until her sister calmed down before she picked the bedroom lock. It was usually in the middle of the night when she was sure her sister was sound asleep, and then Martha could quietly climb to the top bunk. Now didn't seem the time to tell Herman the story, so she just let him fiddle with the small pin in his bulky hands.

Finally, Herman popped the lock. They pushed the door open, flipped the light switch. No Josie. They stepped in and looked around. Dumbfounded as to why they were both in the bathroom. Then Herman saw that her toothbrush was gone.

"She's run away." Herman said like he just figured it out.

"That's nonsense, Herman!"

Herman pointed to her missing toothbrush. Martha gasped and covered her mouth then tears began to stream down her cheeks. "I'll call the Department," Herman said as he walked out of the bathroom, leaving Martha frozen and in tears.

# 12

Josie had quickly walked to her school. She found an open window in one of the classrooms and slithered through it to take a nap someplace warm before she continued on. She curled up in the kindergarten room, where they had mats and blankets.

Ms. Brown would not be pleased to find her there, so she made sure to look at the clock every time the loud clunky radiator turned on and off, which seem to be about every half hour. Her grandmother never used an alarm clock but got up at exactly the same time every day. Josie figured it was a skill she may have inherited too, so she trusted she would wake up before the janitor arrived at seven. She was sure that was at seven and never earlier. Before all the dreams and the house full of so many crime stories, there was almost a year when Josie was in the first grade that her mom had to be at work by seven. So Martha would drop Josie off in front of the school, and Josie wait for Mr. Simpson to arrive in his loud diesel truck — always beating the daycare woman who was perpetually late. Josie was sure the truck would wake her up if her grandmother's trick did not work.

## Sparrow Street

Herman was on the phone while awkwardly getting dressed down in the kitchen, juggling the phone on his ear as he reached to pull his pants on. Martha paced and bit her nails. Still in her pajamas and slippers, she picked up her keys and tossed on her winter coat and gestured to Herman that she was leaving to go look for Josie. Herman covered the receiver with his hand, "You need to wait for an officer to arrive in case she comes home. We don't want her coming back to an empty house."

"She left, Herman. I think she can let herself back in if no one is here. I think she's smart enough to know we're out looking for her. I'm beginning to think she's smarter than both of us."

Herman shook his head at Martha as he responded to Lieutenant Gray on the phone, "Yes, sir. I will. I was going to come in and get a different state car anyways. My radio is on the fritz, and I don't want to be out of touch." He eagerly welcomed the force's help this time. Herman had no idea where Josie would be.

## Kindergarten Classroom

Josie woke up gasping for air and feeling smothered with a cloth again like when she was kidnapped. She had seen her kidnapper in her dream. She saw who it had been in the bathroom. She knew the dress. She jumped up sweating and in a panic. She had to get further away from home. It was almost seven and nearly light out. She needed to find her way to the woods outside of town and take the back roads south. He wouldn't look for her south. She had only taken family vacations north and most of her cousins lived to the west. She had to get out of Michigan. She couldn't trust the Michigan police. She thought maybe she could go to Chicago. Josie and her grandmother had taken a train there once. She needed to find that train.

Meanwhile, Martha was in her car zigzagging through each neighborhood Josie had ever been to. She knew Josie loved hiding in trees, and so she was taking note of low branches while driving slowly and looking up. A car came flooring out of a driveway and didn't see Martha slowly passing by. The driver smashed directly into her passenger side front corner.

Martha jumped out in her slippers with her jacket open, flapping in the cold wind and exposing her pajamas, and said, "Don't call the police!"

"Oh! I'm so sorry I hit you. Are you alright, Miss?" the tall and slender man asked as he approached Martha.

"My daughter is missing, and I don't want any cops coming here when they should be looking for her. So can we settle this later? I need to keep looking," Martha said distractedly as she walked around to look at the damage. "I think my car will drive just fine."

"Your daughter is missing? How long?" the driver calmly asked as he kicked Martha's tire to make sure it wouldn't fall off.

"I don't know, we woke up and she was gone!" Martha held back tears when she said the word gone.

He politely touched her arm to comfort her. "I can help look for her. I am a retired FBI agent. Do you have a photo?"

As Martha rummaged through her wallet she said, "You look young to be retired... here it is," Martha pulled out the photo she had given to the news crews when Josie was kidnapped and handed it over.

He gasped when he saw the photo. "She was the one on the news with psychic powers. Did someone take her again?"

"I think she ran away, or the kidnapper made it look that way. But I think she knows something she doesn't want to tell us. She's been so quiet and withdrawn. Not like herself at all."

"Okay, is there anywhere I should start looking?"

"Maybe the grade school." Martha shook her head. "I just don't know."

"The schools a good place to start. How should I get in touch with you if I find her?"

Martha liked his optimism. He was calm and kind, unlike the dozen officers in her house who seemed more interested in what food Martha had in the fridge and getting the bad guy, not focused on returning her daughter sane and safe. She scribbled her number and name on a piece of paper and the Department number too. "Call the station first, they'll be in direct contact with my husband. He'll have a radio."

"Thanks Martha," he said glancing up from the note. "Now, let's get looking," he encouraged Martha to start moving since she looked frozen in fear. Once he started back towards his car, he then turned back and politely added, "I'm sorry about your car. We *will* settle that later." He walked back and handed Martha his card. "Here's my number in case we don't meet up later. Please let me know if you find her."

Martha nodded, but couldn't find any words as she got back into her car. There was a strange noise in the right front wheel well but Martha kept on driving and looking up each tree. She wondered if that man was going to skip whatever he was going to do. She realized she didn't even get his name. Why did she trust him so quickly? Was it because he looked like her high school sweetheart? Who really was a very plain clean-cut Irish Catholic boy, with very few unique features that stood out. She glanced at the card; it said Steven Collins. Josie was good with strangers. Not Martha, she was good with patients. If they were hurt and needed fixing she could talk to them. This kind stranger made Martha feel flustered, but not uncomfortable. Maybe it was Herman always telling Josie not to talk to strangers that had made Martha distrust people too. She wanted to trust this man. Would he find her sweet Josie? He needed to because her tree strategy seemed to be failing.

She thought it was late enough now to stop at Danny and Adam's houses. Pulling her coat tightly closed, concealing her pajamas, she tried to compose herself as she knocked on each door. She tried to forget she was standing in her slippers and to think instead about Josie's sweet smile. Neither Danny nor Adam had seen her, but they both put on their rubber boots and raced into their backyards the minute they saw Martha at the door. Their parents stood dumbfounded and watched them rummage through the bushes. Danny's mom eventually started yelling, "What on earth are you doing? Get back here."

Danny and Adam had checked the secret boxes for any notes from Josie. There were no notes, but Danny handed Martha some drawings. Martha shook her head and said, "I can't look at those now, please keep them and I'll come back for them."

She asked the boys if there was a box in her backyard. They both nodded in unison. She told them to go look inside it and show the police at the house if they found anything. They gladly agreed and took off in a full sprint towards the Banks' home. Adam and Danny rustled through the bushes around Josie's favorite lilac bush and opened the large box. They shuffled through stacks of paintings of Herman, but there was no note. They handed the large stack to Johnson at the house. Johnson looked puzzled. "These are Josie's secret stash of paintings. Her mom told us to give them to you. We didn't find a note." The boys ran off and Johnson looked through the frenzied drawings of his best friend from grade school. They barely resembled him or a human in some cases. He didn't want Herman to see them so he stashed them in the trunk of his personal car.

Having had no luck at Adam and Danny's, Martha moved on to Yvonne's house. Yvonne had already left for school, but her father said he would send out a search party of his own. Martha envisioned Italian gangsters swooping up Josie from someone's garage or shed. She wasn't sure she trusted the police or Herman to find Josie this time, so she welcomed the help. She thanked Yvonne's father and then hurried down the front stoop stairs, pausing at the bottom and saying, "No guns please. I don't want anyone getting hurt." Yvonne's dad nodded in a steely way, which gave Martha the chills.

## The Department

The chief sent out officers in pairs, and Herman was paired with Johnson. They had a grid system with marked areas on the map where each pair would search in the county. Herman had been part of many search parties. He was shaking because he knew they usually turned up empty. The Department was convinced she couldn't have gotten too far on foot. And Herman was pretty sure Josie wouldn't hitchhike and hadn't been picked up by any relatives. Herman had made calls to all of them to keep a look out. It was a short list. The Banks family was small. Martha's family was in Ohio, and Josie had only met them a few times.

"I don't have any sense where she could've gone. She's been so distant lately," Herman said to Johnson although he wasn't sure that was a completely true statement. He himself had been distant. He knew that much.

"Herman, you found her once — we'll do it again."

"That was different," Herman mumbled.

"I guess last time you got into the head of the kidnapper. This time we're trying to figure out what a nine year old would do. Are you sure she wasn't taken?" Johnson asked.

"I'm sure." Herman said firmly like he was certain. Johnson had a strange feeling about his tone. "Unless the kidnapper let her pack all the peanut butter in the house and let her pack her toothbrush too." Herman sighed. "Her favorite clothes are missing, too. It all seemed too planned out. I didn't have too much time to see what else she took, but my guess is tools or a knife."

"Okay, where would she go?"

"I just said I don't know!" Herman raised his hands off the steering wheel and slammed them back down.

"Okay, the chief has us going north in the county." Johnson read the map and instructed Herman to turn right. They headed out of town.

Hopelessly circling back around, Martha went to the school. The police were there and so was Steven Collins, the man that hit her car. "There is some evidence that she was here," one of the officers said to Martha.

"What kind of evidence?" Martha's first thought was of blood evidence. She was so sick of discussing murder with Herman. This needed to stop. Her mind was full of so much ugliness.

"There seems to be have been someone sleeping in the kindergarten room. Blankets and mats were left out."

Martha took a deep breath. "Ms. Brown would never leave a mess. Neither would Josie unless she was scared. She was obviously more scared of something or someone than of getting yelled at by Ms. Brown. Whose firm discipline had convinced Josie to start cleaning her own room during kindergarten. Something must have really spooked her."

"Okay, well, we have sent another team to search the nearby neighborhoods."

"She *is* smart. She's out of this area fast," Martha insisted.

"Do you have any ideas where she might be headed?" Steven kindly asked.

"My only sense is far away. She's hiding something. Or thinks her life is in danger."

"Okay, I'll go twenty miles out, head back in on the south side of town since the police are working their way out. I'll meet back up with them at some point on the grid," Steven said.

"Who are you again?" the officer asked.

"Retired FBI, Steven Collins." He stuck out his hand but the cop didn't shake it. Just nodded.

Martha was frustrated with how the police were handling the search and liked Steven's attitude. "Can I ride with you?" Martha asked Steven. "That wheel is not going to let me go that far."

"Martha, I'm not sure that's a good idea," the officer said. "You can ride with us around here if you'd like."

"You can radio in my credentials if you'd like. I still have FBI clearance," Steven said.

"That'll take some time, sir, and I'd rather be searching for Josie than looking you up."

"What is your name officer?" Martha asked.

"Smith, Martha. We met when Josie went missing last time," the officer said very politely compared with how he had just addressed Steven.

"I remember. I'm going to go with Mr. Collins. If you'd just take down his license plate I think that should be enough information if I go missing too, don't you think?"

"Sure thing, though I don't like to think of that scenario."

"I'll be fine. Let's just find Josie," Martha said as she climbed into Steven's passenger seat.

⌣

After a couple hours of walking, Josie had gotten tired while she was right in the middle of a plowed cornfield. There was little cover other than a few remaining shriveled cornstalks looking almost deliberately missed by the tractor. She had been crunching across the field, stumbling over thawing dirt mounds and feeling more and more like the little girl with the rabbit, found dead in the field. Although it had crossed her mind, she was glad she didn't bring Tabby along. Josie sat still, cross-legged on the ground, and remembered the Indian play they put on for Thanksgiving at school in first grade. She wanted to be the little Indian girl, but she was the tallest in her class, so she had to be the Pilgrim mother who took in the orphaned Indian girl. Josie's mind slowly quieted down, and she softly laid down and fell asleep.

After what felt like hours, Josie drifted back to consciousness when she heard footsteps. A young boy had spotted Josie in the field and ran over to her without even telling his mother where he was going. As the footsteps got closer, she opened her eyes but did not move. She had seen Tabby do this trick with a bird in the yard. Josie wasn't sure if she was going to have to pounce or run, but she knew her best advantage was stillness. As she saw a pair of small feet getting closer, she took a deep breath and slowly raised her gaze to see a small boy smiling at her. His eyes twinkled like he just had found a treasure.

He plopped down next to her in the dirt and asked, "What are you doing out here? This is so cool to find you."

"You know who I am?" Josie wondered how such a young little boy — he looked half her age — could remember her.

"You're the girl on the news with secret powers."

"I don't have secret powers. Just dreams."

"I have dreams, but I never remember them."

"I couldn't before either."

"So why are you hiding here?"

"You can't tell anyone that you found me." Josie said sternly.

"Oh, I won't," he said with a convincing big kid tone. "But my dad will be home soon, so you need to hide over there by the pine trees. He likes to run the dogs out in the field after work."

"I need to go further than those woods. Do you know where the train station is?"

"You're going that far away?"

"I'm going to…" Josie paused and repeated, "Do you know where the station is?"

"I know where the train tracks are." He got up and pointed. "I see the passenger train going by on it. You could follow the tracks to the next town. I think they have a station."

"Can you take me to the tracks?"

"Yeah, let's go!"

The thawing field made each step forward through the mud an exhausting task. Josie tailed close behind the little boy who was struggling to lift his shoes from the mud. She thought the edge of the farmland look closer when he first pointed towards the pines. After about a football field length of brisk walking the little boy started getting nervous. He paused and looked back towards home. "I might get in trouble for going so far."

"They can't be far now, can't you just take me a bit further?" Josie coaxed him and he nodded. Josie felt bad she was pushing him to go acres from home, but she figured this was her best chance to get to Chicago.

The boy stopped abruptly and pointed. "There. Do you see them?" Before Josie even said yes, the boy had turned and started running home. Josie paused and wondered which way she should go to get to the next town. She looked left where the tracks seemed to curve back towards home and to the right she could see straight down towards what look like buildings in the distance. She decided to head to the right, she felt something familiar about those buildings.

With big steps, almost leaping from one wood tie to the next, she walked for miles along the outside of the train tracks.

## The Search Party

Martha and Steven slowly weaved back into town from twenty miles out. They didn't run into the search party and seemed to have gotten lost on the country roads. As they stopped to look at a map, Martha wondered if Josie was lost and scared. She gazed out the window and realized it was always her who was scared, and how fearless Josie usually was. She wondered who she got that fearlessness from? As they got back on a more direct route back into town, Steven kept saying they should have met up with the search party by now, and how incompetent the police in this area really were. Not saying much, Martha half-listened. She had heard enough complaints about cops messing up crucial evidence at a crime scene from Herman. She wondered why it was called a search party, why party? This was no party.

Without success and many hours of circling the county, Steven dropped Martha at her car. Martha somberly opened the door and thanked him in a monotone voice. He was still optimistic. "I am going to get the FBI involved more heavily on this. We *will* find her, Martha," Steven said.

Martha shook her head and mumbled, "I know. It's just I sense that even when we do, everything will be different." It was starting to get dark, and Martha thought that maybe Josie was hiding close by so she could return to the school after dark. So Martha sat in the school parking lot in her car and prayed.

Praying was not something Martha was accustomed to doing. Her mother had jammed religion down her throat as a child, and she had stopped going to church by the time Josie was born. Josie was magical; there was no need for religion once she was in Martha's life. It was like having a guru in her house all the time. Josie loved to play and laugh, sometimes in the middle of the night. Martha didn't mind. It was Josie's giggle that melted Martha's heart. It wasn't until Herman started working for the Bridgeport Lab that Josie's personality turned serious. Martha sat in her car and thought that if she found Josie, she would need to leave Herman. She wanted to her joyful little girl back.

Martha looked up at the school. Everyone had left and it was dark inside and out. Martha clumsily fiddled around in the back seat, feeling for her flashlight. "It's gone!" Martha gasped. Josie had dropped hers in the water during the flood, and she would never go anywhere in the dark without a flashlight. Martha wept. Completely convinced Josie was not kidnapped, she cried with a sense of relief until her chest tightened again. She started the car to keep looking.

# 13

When Martha entered her house it looked like police headquarters, and she demanded that everyone leave. "This is
our home, and I won't have Josie returning with it looking
like this. This is not a crime scene. Please, everyone out!"

Herman tried to reason with her — telling her that it
was necessary they stay. Martha wouldn't even look at him.

"She left because of all of you. Now go!" she demanded again.

"But she may have been kidnapped and they may contact us here," Herman pleaded.

"She was not kidnapped!" The chatter in the room
stopped and everyone looked at Martha. "The flashlight is
missing from my car. She took it. She knows what she's doing. I have a feeling it has something to do with one of you!"
she said and looked around the room at the men as if they
were all small children caught with their mouths full of the
last cookie.

The chief calmly tried to convince Martha that a cop
could have staged the situation to make it look like Josie ran
away. "He would know to take a flashlight. He would know
to take her favorite foods. I'm not sure she would take her

toothbrush all on her own. I'm sure my little girl would be happy not to brush her teeth. That's what makes me suspect she was taken. And Herman agrees."

Martha glared at the chief and didn't say a word. She thought if she stood still like a wall, his words wouldn't get into her head. She couldn't imagine Josie being kidnapped again. After several minutes of silence, the chief asked everyone to clear out.

Herman quietly said goodnight to the crowd gathered by the door. He apologized for Martha's outburst and thanked the officers for all their help. "Chief, I'll leave the radio on all night. Thanks for trying to talk to Martha. I'm sorry about this."

"This is a horrible situation. She just needs some sleep." The chief shook Herman's hand. "Now don't forget to call if you receive any strange phone calls."

"I won't forget, and I'll join the search party at dawn."

As Herman closed the door, he expected Martha to scream at him. But she was sitting silently in a living room formal chair, hands tightly clasped and resting on her crossed legs. Based on her expression she was hardly in the room at all.

"Martha, are you okay?" Herman said from across the room, still fearful she would lash out.

Martha took a deep breath. "If we find her, I'm leaving," Martha firmly said and didn't change her gaze to look at Herman. She continued to stare out the dark window while Herman sat silently across the room. "She can't be around all this violence anymore. I don't think you're going to quit your job, and I wouldn't ask you to. Your job seems to be more important than your family."

"That's just not true." Herman said defensively.

"I don't think you can see the reality you have created here. You're obsessed with murder. Now our daughter is missing, *again* and obsessed with murder, listening to the police scanner instead of playing with her friends. I want her to have a normal life. This is not normal." Martha had turned towards Herman and glared at him. Her eyes were dark with anger and fear.

"I've done all of this for you and Josie! You wanted a family and house. You got both. I work to provide for you and for her. I choose to solve crimes to protect you both. To keep you both safe."

"If that's the case, why isn't Josie home safe?"

"That's not fair. I didn't do this."

"I think you did. You liked that she could solve crimes. I watched you encourage her to use her gift. I think she knows something that she's afraid to tell you."

"That's absurd. For one there isn't an ounce of fear in that girl. She was out looking at a crime scene in the dark with a flashlight. She wants to be involved more. I am no longer encouraging her and she is still drawing crime scenes. She's not normal and can't be normal. You said it yourself. She has a gift. I didn't give her the gift. I wish she was normal too. I'd do anything to just have a normal family without the news lurking in our front yard like we are freaks or criminals." Herman's voice was getting increasingly louder. Martha retreated into her shell, went silent, and returned her gaze out the window, wondering what normal looked like for Herman.

Herman huffed off. Tossing his arms up in defeat, and went upstairs. Martha reluctantly rose and followed. She could barely stand. She needed to sleep.

## The Train Station

As dusk set in, Josie reached in her raincoat pocket and mindlessly click the flashlight on and off. She feared shining it on the tracks would draw even more attention to the fact that she was someone small traveling alone. While fiddling in her pocket, she felt the ribbed button below her thumb; she tried to remember the story her grandmother told her about the prince. How did it start, was he a boy lost in the woods or out hunting? I think it was hunting. Then he got lost in the woods. Now I remember, he was following a beautiful deer going deeper and deeper into the ancient forest. Josie mind wandered to her grandmother's soft voice and the dramatic way she told the story, pausing after each sentence.

So intent is he upon the hunt that he loses track of the time and, when finally he realizes the day is ending, he is lost, so far from the familiar that, even if he had time to return to his horse before dark, he has no sense of the direction in which to go; and as night falls, he stops in his tracks, frightened of this dark so deep that he is unable to discern even faintly a track to follow.

The prince stands there, torn between this fear and his need — so many people back in his kingdom who depend upon him, who need his leadership, so much that his father had asked of him still undone. But he finds he cannot move, and he remains there, petrified in the dark for one hour, then two, the sounds of the forest growing louder around him, the animals inching closer, becoming more and more bold as the dark of the night thickens.

Finally he moves because he absolutely must. And as soon as he raises his foot and sets it forward, a path appears before him, shining as if in the brightest moonlight. So shocked is the prince that he stops again. And when he stops, the path disappears, and in the sudden, ringing darkness, once again, the predators begin to move in towards him. And driven by fear and responsibility, he takes another step, and the path once again shines forth in the forest, he takes another step, and another. Each time he falters, unsure of where the next turn of the path may take him, the path begins to fade away and he forces himself to take the next step, into the unknown beyond the next curve, and in this way, of course, he is led out of the forest darkness, back to his horse and from there, now free of the oppression of the woods, back to his castle and his kingdom and the love of his people and the meaningful life awaiting him there.

Josie took one step after another as the moon illuminated the metal tracks. With the silent woods closing in on all sides, she tightly held onto the flashlight in her pocket and remembered the prince's bravery. When Josie saw the bright glow of the Amtrak sign, she picked up her pace and breathed deeper than she had for miles.

The building was too lit up, she knew she would need to go up under the dark trees and wait out of sight until the morning train. First she sat in the lawn and made a peanut butter sandwich, and after swallowing it in only a few bites, she took the chef's knife again and spread a ridiculously large amount of peanut butter onto a second sandwich. After the first bite, her mouth nearly sealed shut. The peanut butter on the roof of her mouth had suctioned tightly with her tongue. She hadn't brought anything to drink. She heard her mother's voice in her head saying, "That is way too much peanut butter." Her eyes filled with tears — she missed her mom. And at that moment, she realized she had left her mom with a killer.

She looked for a better place to hide and was lured up the hill by the smell of pine. Josie padded down the pine needles, clearing a spot under a tree, one like hers at home that she pretended was a fort. She wished she remembered her sleeping bag. Her mind swirled around looking out into the darkness. She closed her eyes and sleep took over.

*"Josie, you need to wake up. It's not safe here anymore. They'll find you here."* Josie opened her eyes. No one was there, but she could smell her grandmother's perfume. She saw a cop car in the distance, shining its spotlight around in the dark corners outside the train station. Josie crawled further back into the woods and realized too late that she had left the knife in the lawn. When the cop directed the spotlight in its direction the metal reflected back to him, a luminous spot in the darkness. He stopped the car and searched in the lawn down below the trees. He expected to find the kitchen knife covered in blood, but saw that it was coated with peanut butter. He yelled out, "Josie! Josie are you here?" Josie realized that it was Johnson, but she wasn't sure she could trust him. She tried not to breathe.

She saw that Johnson was headed back to the car. She took a deep breath and thought she was safe. But then he sat down in the driver's seat with the door propped open. She heard him on the radio.

"I think Josie may have gotten on the Amtrak. We need to contact Amtrak. Let's get some officers on the trains and contact Chicago to be on the lookout." Johnson's voice carried up to Josie through the darkness.

Josie didn't know what to do. Now they would be looking for her in Chicago. It was possible they would even send Michigan cops on the trains.

There was nothing else to do, she had to trust Johnson. It was her only chance to keep this search going and figure out a plan to turn in her father. Maybe Johnson could go pick up her mom and then take them both someplace safe. She waited for him to get back out of the car, which for some reason she knew he would do. She wondered if her grandmother's gift was transferring to her.

She quietly gathered her things, still unsure, and approached Johnson from behind. He turned around when he heard her shuffling tired feet. "Josie, thank god you're okay!" Johnson bent down to hug her. His face was lined with relief and exhaustion.

"You can't tell anyone. You can't tell my dad," Josie abruptly said as Johnson tried to hug her.

"But Josie, they're worried to death. I have to take you home."

"You can't. My dad is a killer." Josie blurted out but at the same time wanted to pull the words back in. She didn't want it to be true.

"What are you saying?" Johnson bent down and looked into Josie's tearful eyes. "Maybe your dream was wrong. I know your dad. I've known him since he was your age. He's no killer."

Josie wiped away her tears and firmly said, "He was the kidnapper that took me from school."

"What? That's not possible."

"How did he find me? I saw his hands and shoes moments before he grabbed me. It was him."

"But you said it was a woman you saw in the bathroom that day."

"He was wearing one of my grandmother's dresses."

"Jo are you sure?"

Josie nodded. Only her dad called her Jo. It made her feel closer to Johnson when he said it, but also gave her the shivers.

"What do you mean he's a killer?" Johnson was confused how the kidnapping and murder were connected.

"I'm scared." Josie wasn't sure whether she had done the right thing.

"Okay, let's get you someplace warm and safe. I'll contact the chief."

"No! We need to go to the FBI or Chicago police. We *can't* go to Bridgeport."

"Okay, we'll go to the FBI Headquarters."

"Can we pick up my mom? I think she may be in danger."

"Josie, are you sure?"

Josie nodded as tears streamed down her face. She was scared her dad had hurt her mom. All of her dreams had her mom in trouble in the upstairs hallway.

"It's okay, Jo. It'll all be okay. I believe you." Josie hugged him tightly. "I need to get Herman out of the house first. I'll put you someplace safe, call in Herman, and then go pick up Martha," Johnson said out loud as though reciting a grocery list, not really talking to Josie.

As Johnson dropped Josie off at his hunting cabin thirty miles north of Saginaw he reassured her, "You'll be safe here." Josie nodded. "Lock the door when I leave." Josie nodded again.

He had a dreadful feeling that somehow they would find her there and think he took her. He had to hurry. He turned to channel 2 and radioed the Department. He told them he was bringing in the knife he had found, and they should call Herman in to confirm that it was theirs.

"I could go to the house but Martha was pretty upset we were there, so I thought Herman coming to the Lab would be better," he said into the Motorola receiver, trying to keep his voice steady and convincing.

"Well, I don't know. This seems like a whole lot of extra steps. Going straight to the house would be faster. However, if you think this way is best then fine," said Lieutenant Gray.

Johnson then had to figure out how he would negotiate not waiting to show Herman the knife himself. As he frantically drove he thought up different excuses.

After making record time to Bridgeport, he dropped off the knife, leaving it in an evidence bag in the Lab. He told the officer on night duty his wife was not feeling well, and he needed to get home. His wife had actually left him a few months back when he was spending every night at the Banks' house. He hoped no one had found out yet.

Slipping out the back door, Johnson took his personal car from the lot, sped across Dixie Highway to Saginaw and waited near the Banks' home. When he saw Herman's car leave the driveway, he waited a few minutes and then he approached the house on foot. He thought maybe he'd have to break in if the house was all dark and Martha was asleep. He thought about loudly knocking on the back door, but he was afraid it was going to scare her, and she'd call the police. So he picked the lock and snuck in the kitchen door. He tiptoed upstairs and found Martha pointing a gun down the hall at him.

"Martha, don't shoot. It's Johnson." In the dark Johnson lost his footing and seemed to lurch towards her. "I have Josie at…"

"You're the kidnapper! You're the killer Josie is afraid of in her own house! I trusted you! How could you?" Martha cocked the gun and closed her eyes.

"No! Don't…" Johnson cried out as Martha fired.

## The Hunting Cabin

Josie knew something was wrong when she saw the sun glaring through the windows. She squinted and heard her grandmother's voice saying, "Mind your dreams. They do not lie." She didn't remember having a dream last night. Though her grandmother's voice lingered in her mind almost trying to convince her that she had done the right thing.

She wasn't sure how long she had been sleeping. The cabin was cozy and the bed had lots of heavy blankets stacked high. After peering out the frosted window she crawled back under and pulled the covers up to her nose, and took a deep breath like her grandmother told her to do when she was scared. The weight of blankets on her chest made her feel safe. She missed Tabby. Maybe Johnson grabbed Tabby too, she thought. She laughed thinking about Tabby under Johnson's arm getting into the squad car. Cop Cat she would call her.

When Josie opened her eyes hours later, her stomach growled. She pried the covers off and went to the scratched-up little table by the door where she had left her things and made another peanut butter sandwich. She had a feeling she might have to ration her supplies. She looked around in the cupboards. They were a bit bare, stocked with cans of beans. Josie didn't like beans.

Motionless, she looked out the window, staring into hundreds of skinny pines. It looked cold and damp. She couldn't remember seeing any stores for miles down on the paved road. The trees looked like a maze. She wasn't even sure which way the road was.

## Sparrow Street

Now her home really was a crime scene, Martha thought. She sat paralyzed in the same chair she had sat in when she told Herman she was leaving. Frozen, she didn't know if she could even leave the chair, let alone leave Herman now. She herself had brought violence into the home. Now she was just like Herman. How would she be able to tell the courts she wanted sole custody of her daughter when she was a killer?

The atmosphere in the house was oppressive. It was uncomfortably silent at times with a few officers rustling around collecting evidence. The officers had lost one of their own, yet they were all dedicated to helping the Banks family. Lieutenant Gray took special care when he interviewed her. He was concerned that the pieces weren't fitting together. He had a hard time thinking of Johnson as the killer, but he also knew Johnson had just lied to him. It all looked fishy. Herman's eyes darted around the room, though he stood completely still and silent next to Martha while Gray asked her questions. He then randomly started pacing, breaking his immobile stance, and blurted out, "We still need to find Josie!"

## The Hunting Cabin

Several days had passed since Johnson left Josie in the cabin. She had been wearing the same dirty clothes, even to bed, in anticipation of leaving at any moment. Josie was confused about what could have gone wrong with the plan. She was avoiding sleeping, restless and up most of the night. Had Johnson told her dad everything? What has happened to Johnson? She didn't want to think about it. Her gut told her that Johnson was dead, but she didn't dare dwell on it. She tried to sleep as little as possible, so she wouldn't dream about it. She was reluctant to leave the cabin and adjacent woods, but she would need supplies soon. Surrounded by the trees she felt safe, but she had to figure out how to get her mom there too. She couldn't call because her home phone was likely tapped. They did that when she was kidnapped. So she hung out in the woods, never straying far. Whittling away as many hours as possible, she collected sticks to pin up her knotted hair up, climbed trees, and tried to imagine liking beans, which was going to be her next meal.

## The Department

The FBI got heavily involved once Johnson was killed. They searched his house and brought his wife back from Louisiana to question her. Mrs. Johnson said she had left because he had grown overly concerned with helping the Banks. "He was getting more and more attached to Josie since we learned we were unable to have kids," she said tearfully. The officers took this as a sign that he was possibly the first kidnapper. Johnson's wife asked if they had searched his hunting cabin yet. "He went there a lot even during the off season. I wasn't sure what he was doing up there."

Herman made a good case that he should come with the FBI search team. "If Johnson took her, she might be extremely frightened of cops. You might need me there to coax her out. I don't want her feeling like she is being kidnapped again," he pleaded in a fatherly tone.

Upon arrival at the cabin, the FBI walked around the perimeter and saw signs of small footprints. They were pretty sure Josie was in there. So they let Herman go in first.

Herman cracked open the door. "Josie? It's your dad, you in here?"

Josie came running, "Dad!"

"Josie! I'm so glad you are safe! I love you so much." Herman grabbed and hugged her tighter.

"I love you too, Dad." Joy leaped across Josie's face, and then her features sank in fear.

"What happened to Johnson?" Josie said and loosened herself from her dad's hug.

"It's over now Josie. Johnson is dead." Herman squeezed her harder.

"What? Did you kill him?" Josie pulled away. The lead FBI agent, Steven's old partner, overheard Josie and perked up.

"No, Josie that's not what happened. I'm glad you're safe. Let's get you home and fed. Your mom will be *so* happy to see you."

"But Johnson was supposed to…"

"It's all over now." Herman interrupted and squeezed her tightly. Josie's face wrinkled with fear. The lead agent took note.

Josie rode home with her dad and the lead agent in an unmarked car. Josie didn't say much. The agent tried to ask a few questions, but each time Herman said, "Now is not the time." Josie nodded in agreement with her father but made sure to be nice to the agent. He didn't seem to like her dad nor even know his name first name, harshly addressing him only as Mr. Banks.

When they pulled into the Bank's driveway, Josie saw her mom sitting by the window, draped in blankets, looking frozen. Josie nearly leapt out of the car before it stopped rolling.

Josie ran inside to her mom, throwing her arms around her before Martha even had a moment to respond. Josie asked, "Are you okay? Are you okay?"

"Oh, sweet Josie, are you okay? I'm fine."

"You looked so sad in the window."

"I'm happy now. You're safe." Martha was happy though her face was swollen from tears. She agonized over what she had done. She hoped Josie hadn't dreamt about it.

"You haven't had any dreams about me, have you Josie?" Martha asked in a shaking voice.

"Yes, you were in danger in a hallway and I wanted to help you."

Martha sobbed and prayed Josie would never see what really happened in that hallway, but slowly Josie's dreams revealed the shooting.

# 14

In the following weeks, Martha made it a habit to get up early when the house was quiet. It was the only time she felt peaceful. She sat perfectly still looking out the window for hours with her hands molded around a cup of hot tea. She was doing exactly this one morning in May, and she was thinking about Steven, the man who crashed into her car.

She couldn't put her finger on what it was about him. His eyes were so much kinder than other agents and officers she had met over the years. He was such a big support when Josie had gone missing again, Martha thought. She needed a touch of kindness. After Johnson's shooting and with Josie safely home, the police force had ostracized their family. Traumatized by the shooting, she had made a pact with Herman not to talk about it ever again. She had become ambivalent about leaving Herman, and needed someone objective to talk to. Steven was the only person who wasn't connected to their family or friends. Martha decided to call him once Herman left for work.

Steven and Martha had met a few weeks earlier at the insurance office to settle the car accident details and ended up talking for quite awhile in the parking lot. They talked mostly about Josie. Now Martha wanted to talk about life, not crime, not just Josie. So much of the past year had been taken up with what Josie had needed. Martha needed a friend. This time Martha picked a more casual location, Hoyt Park, to meet with Steven – and she also brought Josie along. Josie quickly took to Steven.

"So you work for the FBI? How cool." Josie smiled. "I worked for them in the past. I'm retired now."

"But you look so young," Martha chimed in.

"Well, I suppose I am. It's a long story, for another time."

"So you know a lot about protective custody?" Josie asked.

"I do."

"Well, how long do you need to be in it, and do they move you to another state?" "Why are you so curious about needing protection, Josie?"

Martha interrupted and crouched down to look Josie in the eyes. "Josie, Johnson is dead. That's all over. You're safe now."

"I know," Josie said as she took a breath to begin to tell them the whole story, but then she fell silent. She didn't think her mom was ready to hear that she was living with the real kidnapper and a killer.

Although Steven noticed Josie's pause and glanced at her mom. Martha didn't seem to take note of Josie's need to say something. "Josie, do you want a tour of the FBI Head-quarters?" Steven asked.

"Yes!" Josie jumped up and then glanced back at her mom, who was frowning. Martha didn't like the idea but was happy that Steven had changed the subject.

"Well, maybe one day while your mom is at work, after school I can take you."

"Tomorrow?" Josie pleaded. She needed to get her mom out of that house. The tension was building between her parents. Nightly, Josie overheard them having spats behind their closed bedroom door.

Martha looked nervously at Steven. "I'm not sure that's a good idea." Martha had a bad feeling in the pit of her stomach that Herman would be furious if he found out. This adventure to the park was even a risk but crossing the line with Herman's work would definitely cause a fight.

"Why Mom? I won't tell Dad I'm going."

Martha paused and looked Josie in the eyes. Martha had a familiar feeling, like she used to get with Herman's mother when she was reading her mind and answering her questions before she spoke them out loud. Martha had been denying Josie's powerful talents, and she needed to find a way to trust again. She needed to allow Josie to be magical again. "I don't have to work tomorrow, so I can bring her to Headquarters. I'm not sure Herman would like Josie driving around in a car with a man he doesn't know. He still doesn't know that I was." Josie jumped up and down grinning and cheering as Martha smiled at Steven.

"Gotta love the cop code of silence. No one was going to tell him, because then someone would have been accountable for letting you go with me."

"Let's not talk about cops," Martha requested. "Can we just have a lovely walk by the river?"

"Of course. This park is one of my favorite places in town," Steven said and smiled to lighten the mood.

"Josie's too." Martha said as she nervously glanced over to see where Josie had run off. Josie had found her way down the hill to the banks of the Saginaw River by a few fishermen. Martha thought of calling her to come back up the hill, but she was enjoying being alone with Steven. She felt safe with him. Herman's anger and aggression seemed even more extreme now that Josie was safe. Martha assumed it was because of her killing Johnson. She was convinced that Herman was repulsed to be living with a killer, since he had dedicated his life to putting them in prison.

Down by the river, Josie asked one of the men if she could cast with his fishing rod. The man scowled and grumbled as he reluctantly handed her the pole. His bucket of fish was slim, just one small perch.

"Can I put a fresh worm on it?"

"You know a lot about fishing for such a little girl," he said as he handed her the container of night crawlers.

"My godparents live on a lake. I've been told I'm a pretty lucky fisherman."

"Well, catch me some dinner then, fisher-girl."

"I like that, *fisher-girl*." Josie said as she cast the line, fumbling with the fishing pole, which was much too large for her.

Martha nudged Steven as she saw Josie toss out the line. "Watch this. She'll catch a fish. She always does. Herman won't take her fishing anymore because the fish never bite his line. She's amazing." Martha smiled as she watched Josie fish.

Josie slowly reeled in her line. The fisherman started to talk, but Josie brought her index finger to her lips and made a soft shhh noise. Josie's arms lurched forward when the fish tugged on the line. The old man stood behind her, grabbed hold of the pole and helped turn the reel. As they drew the fish out of the water, Josie yelled, "It's a walleye!"

The grumpy old man smiled and grabbed the fish, tossing it in his bucket, which was almost too small to contain it. The fish was the size of a football.

Steven and Martha laughed. "She is one special little girl," Steven said.

Martha nodded in agreement then called down to Josie, "Josie! Time to go!"

Josie turned towards them and pointed to the fish.

"We saw the whole thing! Good job pulling it in!" Martha yelled.

"Thank you, sir, for letting me fish," Josie said as she turned to run up the hill.

"No, thank you for catching my dinner," the old man said with a big smile.

Between the uphill jog and her excitement about the fish, she was still gathering her breath. "Mom, I don't want to eat fish anymore. I really like to watch them swim. Catching is fun, but only when we let them go."

"Okay, Josie. We'll talk about it more later."

Slowly, Martha walked back to the car ahead of Steven and Josie, who were talking about fishing. She was happy to hear Josie talking about something other than crimes. Martha gave Steven a faint smile as they said their goodbyes. She didn't want him to know how much she was touched by his closeness with Josie. "I'll see you two tomorrow around 3:30," Steven said with a smile.

## FBI Headquarters

The next afternoon Martha and Josie drove in silence to the FBI Headquarters in Bay City to meet Steven. He was waiting outside chatting with a few agents when they arrived. Josie leapt out of the car. Martha noted her excitement was a bit different than her normal adventures to the Lab with her dad. She seemed eager, a little nervous but then again, Josie was never nervous.

Martha thought about when Josie was around nineteen months old and went up to everyone she saw and asked them if they wanted a snuggle. Snuggle was her word for hug at the time. Rarely did anyone turn down such a request from a cute little girl. Martha tried at first to limit the hugging to family gatherings, and then birthday parties and daycare moms and dads. Then it happened at the grocery store. It was a challenge when Josie would reach her arms out while strapped into the cart and offer other shoppers a snuggle. Martha thought it was pretty harmless, but Herman put a stop to it when they were at a Michigan State basketball game and Josie had wanted to hug everyone all the way to their seats. Herman was frustrated by the prospect of missing the first half. He squatted down to Josie's level, looked her in the eye and said, "No more snuggles!" Josie listened and stopped snuggling. She even stopped offering her dad and mom snuggles and just gave them kisses goodnight instead. Martha missed those hugs.

After Steven, Martha, and Josie had circled around the headquarters' main area, Josie blurted out, "Can I talk to the head FBI agent?"

Steven and Martha glanced at each other with a questioning look.

"The SAC — Oh, I mean the Special Agent in Charge? Of course." Steven smiled.

"Alone?" Josie asked with very little expression on her face and looked at her mom.

"Okay, Josie. I'll wait right here in the lobby." Martha kissed the top of Josie's head. Josie trotted off with Steven down the hall. It took all of Martha's inner strength to let Josie go alone to have this experience. Martha's mind flashed to Josie and Johnson walking off to school. She let it go as best she could.

Still, she couldn't stop herself from calling Josie back from down the hall. When Josie reached her, Martha had a big smile on her face. "May I have a snuggle?"

"Mom, I don't call them that anymore." Josie said while shaking her head.

"I know. You're all grown up. Just indulge me before the FBI offers you a job."

With a big smile Josie, hugged her mom. Martha held on tight and took in a deep breath in of Josie's freshly washed hair. "Have fun, Josie," Martha said as she released her daughter from her arms. Josie flew off towards Steven. With a reassuring glance, Steven smiled back at Martha.

"Can I meet with him in one of those interrogation rooms with no recording?" Josie said as they neared a private entrance.

"How do you know about all this stuff?" Steven didn't press for an explanation. It appeared his hunch was right. Josie was hiding something and clearly wanted to tell someone.

"Oh, my dad talks about it all the time. And the courtroom scenes from *Quincy* of course."

Steven laughed and guided Josie down the hall to the SAC's office. The SAC and Steven had a few words about old times and shared a couple of laughs. Josie stood still with her hands fidgeting behind her back. She glanced at all the books and awards. The Special Agent in Charge didn't look much different from the state cops, Josie thought. He was cleanly shaved, tall, and broad shouldered with a bit of a potbelly, and maybe a bit more gray. When Steven told the SAC what Josie would like to do, there was almost a playful wink between the two men and then the agent said, "Of course, I won't grill you too hard though," while smiling at Josie. Josie didn't quite get the joke but smiled politely back.

Suddenly Josie's mood changed as they headed down an unmarked narrow hallway. The SAC was talking about his grandchildren and all Josie could muster up to say was a few uh-huhs. Josie clenched her jaw and held her arms tightly to her chest when they entered an interrogation room. When the door sealed tightly closed behind them, the SAC looked at her and felt the need to reassure her that everything would be all right. "Do you want to leave? You look upset," he said with concern.

"My father is a murderer," Josie blurted out before they even sat down. "He was the one who kidnapped me, not Johnson."

The agent was taken aback. She was so firm, so serious. He offered her a seat and gently guided her back into the conversation.

"Josie, what you are saying is rather serious. Are you telling stories?"

"No." Josie finally uncrossed her arms and seemed more comfortable talking. "Johnson was going to my house to pick up my mom and bring her to his cabin, so we could get away from my dad. Johnson was going to bring me here, so I could tell *you* everything. Johnson was going to bring me *here*." Josie pressed her finger into the table. She wasn't sure he was going to believe her. Johnson had believed her, though. Johnson had understood that her dreams were correct and once he saw all those strange drawings of Herman, he knew.

"Hold on… does your mom know any of this? I'm confused as to why she shot Johnson."

"I haven't told her anything. She was scared, that's why she shot him. Johnson broke into our house that night. Before that I was still having feelings that the kidnapper was in there, in the house, I mean. That was while Johnson was there, protecting us. I said at one point, 'there is a killer in our house.' This was way before the dreams showed me that my dad was a murderer."

"What do you mean when you say that your father is a murderer?"

"He hung that woman in the barn by our house and that man from the bar in his basement."

"How do you know this?" The director hoped someone was behind the one-way window, seeing what was happening, and had switched on the recorder.

"My dreams. And he took the rope from my room and used it on the man."

"I have heard how accurate your dreams are, Josie, but can you go into more detail? This is a serious matter."

"I don't know where the lady came from, but my dad pulled her out of his state car trunk and dragged her across the field by our house towards the barn. My cat Tabby followed. The woman was limp like a big stuffed animal, but

I'm not sure she was dead. The grass and weeds were tall so he laid her flat on the ground and had the rope around her neck and pulled her."

"So there may be rope burns that are different from the hanging marks," the agent said, thinking out loud to himself.

"He went back for a ladder and pulled it across the field the same way. I think with a different rope though. When I went across the field the next morning I noticed the matted weeds and was just happy there was a trail all the way to the barn, because that was where I was headed to find Tabby. I don't think the cops even went into the field much that day. My mom wouldn't let me watch out of the window, so I don't know for sure."

"I'll look into it."

"Okay." Josie was glad he seemed to believe her now. "My dad made some fancy pulley system, kind of like when he built my tree house. He had hoisted wood up to the high branches with it. It might still be somewhere in our garage. I haven't looked—it's messy in there and full of spiders. I don't like spiders. Well, that's not true. I do like to watch them build their webs but from far away."

"I'm scared of spiders too. But don't tell the guys. They'll tease me."

"Your secret is safe with me," Josie promised. She had made the same promise to Adam and Danny before they all started kindergarten.

"Is there anything else about the woman that you know? Missing persons has nothing. We still don't know who she is." The agent had changed his voice back to a more serious tone.

"I can't see anything else about her. I've tried. She never spoke or anything in my dream. She was just limp. But she has a clump of hair missing from her head. My dad collects hair." Josie turned her head around and showed a hidden little missing patch of her long hair. Tears welled up in her dark eyes.

The agent gently touched her arm. "It's okay, Josie. Do you want to tell me about the man now or take a break?'

"Can I have some hot cocoa?" Josie never got that stuff at home. Lately, her mother had been making her drink herbal tea, which tasted like flowers.

"You got it." The agent left for a moment, and then a young woman brought in hot chocolate for Josie.

"Is he coming back?" Josie asked the woman.

"He'll be right in," she said sweetly.

"Is he calling my dad?"

"Oh, I don't think so. He just had some other work to do real quickly. Don't worry, he hasn't forgotten about you," she said in a comforting tone. Josie liked the lady's leather boots and thought she looked too young to be an agent, and wondered if maybe she had a special talent.

Several agents had a lengthy discussion in the SAC's office about the validity of Josie's dreams. The lead agent who found her in the cabin had been doing research on Herman and about Josie's dreams; Herman had given off a bad vibe, he thought. He had been listening to the state police scanner and had been keeping track of what cases Herman was involved with.

"This isn't about one of your hunches is it, Deerfield?" the SAC asked. Someone else chimed in, at the back of the room, that he didn't believe these dreams were anything more than a little girl's twisted fantasies.

"Well, she is a powerful little girl, not like my grandkids, that's for sure. Thank you for all of your opinions, now let's get looking into the facts of these cases and see if she is telling the truth," the SAC said and motioned with his hand that they all should disperse.

Josie slowly drank half the cup of cocoa before the agent returned. She was getting anxious.

"Did you call my dad?" Josie blurted out when he sat down across the table from her.

"No. That's not how we're going to handle this. We're confirming what you've told us, without your father knowing, and then we'll see what happens." He was reluctant to say the word arrest. He didn't know how comfortable Josie would be to finish the interview knowing it might put her father in prison. "Are you ready to talk about the man? What did you see in your dream?" Josie did a lot of silent nodding.

"I wasn't having any dreams about him at first, until I had the dream about my dad taking my rope and drawings from my room," Josie said after a long pause.

"So you didn't actually see your dad take any of your stuff?"

"He disappeared the night the man was hung, and so did all my stuff from under my bed and in my closet: all of my drawings, the rope, and the lab supplies I had been storing. I think my dad figured out that I knew more than I was saying about the woman in the barn when he caught me with the rope that afternoon."

"I see. So what happened to the man?"

Josie fidgeted in her seat and shyly began to talk again. "I saw that my dad followed him home from a bar... I saw him in my dream. My mom says it's important that I say 'I saw the murders in my dream,' so I don't scare people or get reality and dreams confused."

"That's good advice. So the man was at a bar?"

"Yes, and in the bar the man had been rude to all these women. I think maybe my dad was protecting the girls. He is a nice guy. The man was pretty drunk. His car was swerving all over road in my dream. My dad drove a little behind him. He hates drunk drivers and always points them out on the road and calls them in if we're in the state car."

"What happened on the road that night?" the agent said, trying to keep Josie on track.

"They just drove slowly. But once he pulled into his driveway, the drunk man stood fumbling with his keys to lock the car up and that was when my dad grabbed him from behind. He stuck a long needle in the back of his neck. I don't like needles. Those vaccination shots hurt." Josie tightened up her shoulders and shook her head thinking about needles. "Then he dragged him into the house, not with a rope this time but by his arms. He rolled him down the stairs to the basement. Then he went back to his car and grabbed the rope, went back inside the house and locked the door behind him. It gets fuzzy for a bit. I can't really see what happens until I see the man is pleading and kicking as my dad strings him up over the beam. I don't like to see that part. Can I stop now?"

"Of course. You've been so brave."

"That's what my dad says to me. I don't want to be brave anymore. I want to be a kid."

"What would you like to do the rest of the day? I can arrange any food you'd like to be delivered pizza or Chinese, or we can bring in a TV and you can watch a movie? We have fancy equipment here; it's called a VHS. It plays movies."

Josie wasn't interested in movies right then. She was feeling overwhelmed that she had just broken up her family. The truth meant her dad would go to jail. Her grandmother always told her to tell the truth. She'd say something about how the truth will set you free. Her grandmother was always talking about being free. Josie didn't feel free in this small room, knowing what she had just done to her father.

"Can I see my mom, now?" Josie asked as tears streamed down her cheeks.

"Of course. Anything else you need to tell me? I don't really want you to relive this again, so now is the time."

"The man has a clump of hair missing like the lady. I thought my dad only took girls' hair, but it seems like he used men's too."

"Thank you, Josie."

"I don't know where he hid the hair. He told me mine was used for his lectures and demonstrations. Maybe theirs was too."

"We'll find it, Josie. Don't you worry about it. You don't have to worry anymore. You can let all this go now."

"Okay." But Josie wasn't sure it would be so easy.

"Is your mom still here?"

"She should be in the lobby, probably reading. She's been reading a lot of books lately. That's about all she's been doing. Sometimes she goes to the grocery store but mainly just reading."

"Okay, hang tight. I'm going to send Steven back in to sit with you while I talk with your mom. Don't tell Steven anything yet, okay? We need to keep this a secret, like the spiders, until… well, until I say so. Okay?"

"Okay," Josie said softly as she sank a little further down into the firm office chair.

## The Lab

"Herman, the SAC from the FBI is on the line for you," said the Lab secretary. "Something about unsolved cases, but he wouldn't say more."

Herman grabbed the phone quickly. "Hello, sir."

"Herman, can you come up to headquarters? We need to discuss having Josie on our investigation team. She just helped solve a couple of big unsolved cases for us."

"How did you get a hold of my daughter? Who brought her to you?"

"Well, your wife is here with her." Herman was furious at Martha. He paced and tossed a stapler across the room.

"What's going on here?" Herman questioned.

"I think it was a rather innocent move on your wife's part, having Steven give Josie a tour of our facilities. Then Josie started talking about cases."

"Who the hell is Steven?"

"We'll explain when you get here."

"I need to wrap up a sample here, then I can head over." Herman looked around to see if anyone noticed what a mess the stapler had made when it hit a pile of evidence, scattering it onto the floor. He took a deep breath when he saw no one and remembered everyone was out in the field.

"Of course, do what you need to do." The SAC hung up and turned to the agent in his office. "I want two more men on him, now!" He had already sent two before he made the call, but he had a feeling Herman might flee. However, he was also hoping that Herman was so prideful and protective of his daughter that it would draw him in.

Herman hurried to finish his chemical sperm test for a new rape case the prosecutor wanted rushed through. Then he hurried out, ignoring his secretary's goodbye, and got into a state car. He saw two separate unmarked cars were following him. The tale confirmed his suspicions that Josie had dreams about him. His plan had backfired. He wondered if she had told the FBI agent about the two people he had killed. After Johnson's death, Herman had believed that Josie wouldn't tell. He knew how close they had become and Herman could tell how frightened his daughter was at home since then — frequently asking questions about how Johnson was killed. He drove slowly and berated himself that he shouldn't have planted the hooker's body in the barn so close to home, but he thought the proximity would work to stop her dreams. His thoughts then turned to whether Josie had told them everything, and how he would get out of it. He knew if he wanted to stay out of prison Josie would have to be institutionalized. Deeming her crazy would be his only way out.

He decided he had two choices. One was to walk in head high and tell them his daughter was lying and that she was delusional and having night terrors, thinking she could see the future and past. He could say he had determined that if she thought she was solving crimes, her night terrors decreased. And that he had been lying all along to the press when actually he had fed her information about all of the cases and helped her with all her paintings. This plan would involve getting Martha on his side. He wasn't sure if that was possible.

His other option was to tell the truth.

The SAC met Herman at the front door as the four agents followed closely behind. "Right this way, Herman." The SAC held the door and then gestured to the first room to the right, a smaller interrogation room with two-way mirrors and microphones. He then gestured for Herman to sit on the side facing the reflecting glass window.

Herman had never before sat on this side of the table. He looked around, wanting to inquire where Josie was, but the agent started talking: "Josie has informed us about the circumstances of the murdered woman in the barn and the man hung in his basement. Do you want to elaborate?"

Faintly in his mind, Herman heard his mother's voice saying, "Defense is the first act of war." He couldn't bear to put Josie through any more violence.

"I did it to stop Josie's dreams. I did it to protect her. My mother used to have the same dreams and hers stopped once my brother was killed in a car crash. I thought if the murders were personal, if I was involved in some way like my brother's accident, then Josie's dreams would stop. Those two people had to be murdered so Josie would think I was responsible, and then her dreams would stop. I didn't want my daughter to live a life full of violence and in the spotlight of the press for the rest of her life and seen as a freak like my mother was. She deserves more. I wanted her to have a normal life, study art, and move away from this place. I spend hours looking through microscopes, standing over dead bodies at morgues and in the middle of nowhere, looking for the tiniest clue to put one more murderer away, one more person that can't get anywhere near my little girl. Then the violence came into her mind. It was ruining her life. I had to do something. We had this innocent little girl that brought so much joy into our lives and now all she thinks about is murder. I needed to stop her violent dreams before they destroyed her." Herman said frantically, while sweat accumulated on his forehead. It was all he could do to keep his voice steady.

"Did you murder your brother, too?"

"No. But my mother thought I did. My brother lost control of the car on the ice. As we slid towards the edge of the road where it drops off down into the Flint River I yelled for him to turn into the skid. He turned the wrong way. I grabbed the wheel and the car spun out of control, and we hit the pine trees." Guilt washed over Herman's face, and he darted his glance away from the agent.

———

Josie sat with a second cup of hot chocolate, which was growing cold. She had barely touched it. She silently cried and occasionally gasped for air. The young female agent watched helplessly behind the two-way glass until she couldn't take it any longer then went into the room. She sat close to Josie, hesitating at first, but when Josie didn't react with anything, but a tearful glance, she reached out to hold her.

At the other end of the hall there was a commotion. "Wait, Martha. You can't go in there," Steven yelled after Martha, who paced ahead in a full rage.

Martha burst into the interrogation room where her husband was being held and slipped through the arms of the guard, who attempted to restrain her. "You kidnapped our daughter, your own daughter. You monster! You left her in the dark. How could you?" Martha's voice cracked as the guards pulled at her to get her out of the room. She continued yelling, "Herman, you can't play God. It will not bring her back. Your mother or our innocent child. Everything changes. Not just the things we want. Everything!" Herman sat motionless and speechless as the SAC and guard pulled Martha out of the room and the door slammed.

"Why did you kidnap your daughter?" The SAC asked as he sat back down at the table.

"So the press would release the statement that her drawings were fake. I needed to show everyone how much pain it causes a family when law enforcement uses your daughter or mother to solve crimes. I needed to scare Josie so she would stop…"

"Stop what?"

Herman shook his head.

"Stop using her gift?" the SAC asked. "She is gifted, powerful beyond measure. Could help so many people. Why stop that?"

Herman didn't answer.

When she heard her mom yelling, Josie ran down the hall, her flip-flops pounding on the tile floor. As soon as the agents figured out that the noisy stomping was Josie, they released Martha, and Josie embraced her mom. They both sobbed, while the agents hovered around them, shielding them from view, as Herman was escorted down the hall in handcuffs. "I had to tell, Mom. I had to tell the truth. I know this changes everything. I know I just hurt Dad. But I want you to be free. Grandma always said 'the truth will set you free.'"

# Acknowledgements

I am deeply thankful to my family, first readers, editors, book club members, writers' group, and graphic designers for all their help with *Under the Pines*. A special thank you to Andy Bartolotta, Emma Bilyk, Tim Drescher, Brian Foote, Susan Gilkey, Jenny Hoobler, Ryan Kilpatrick, KB Jensen, Anna Joranger, Matt Millikan, Trisha Olson, David Spratte, and Erin Waser. I'd also like to express the enormous gratitude I have for my teachers Thom Knoles, Jeff Kober, Light Watkins, and Jennifer Hains, whose guidance and wisdom have helped make this book a reality. And I'd like to give a heart-filled thank you to my father for dinner conversations about murder. These words strung together could not have happened without his love of science. It was a pleasure to create this book together with all of you.

54451837R00140

Made in the USA
Lexington, KY
16 August 2016